"A word to the wise, Ms. Johnson."

Sam shook his head. "I have all the dates I want, and when I marry, the bride will be one I select, not one chosen by my female relatives. And she sure as hell won't be a freckle-faced, wildly dressed gypsy with a ready-made family."

"I may have freckles," Addy retorted, "but at least I'm human, which is more than can be said for you."

Dear Reader,

Celebrating the milestones of our lives joyfully affirms the choices we make as we stumble along. A personal milestone is this book, my fifteenth published by Harlequin Romance. In the book, Sam and Addy illustrate a favorite romantic concept of mine—opposites attract.

This year my husband and I will celebrate the thirty-second anniversary of a marriage most people said wouldn't last a week. We differ on religion, political affiliation, music, raising kids, spending money, vacationing, frying eggs, wine and how to eat potatoes. I drink coffee; he drinks tea.

We share love and laughter.

For Sam and Addy, and for you, I wish the same sustaining love and laughter.

Jeanne Allan

Needed: One Dad
Jeanne Allan

Harlequin Books

TORONTO • NEW YORK • LONDON
AMSTERDAM • PARIS • SYDNEY • HAMBURG
STOCKHOLM • ATHENS • TOKYO • MILAN
MADRID • WARSAW • BUDAPEST • AUCKLAND

For my aunts, D, E and C.
Thanks.

ISBN 0-373-03456-3

NEEDED: ONE DAD

First North American Publication 1997.

Copyright © 1997 by Jeanne Allan.

CHAPTER ONE

"SAM! Where are you? I want you. Can you hear me?"

Addy shook her head tolerantly. The warm July day meant wide-open windows in the old Victorian house, and no doubt the whole of Ute Pass heard Emilie shouting to her toy bear. Addy picked up a sharp surgical blade to slice off a thin slab of the angel-patterned polymer clay cane for the bead she was making.

"I'm Sam. Who are you and what do you want me for?"

In the all-female household, the deep, male voice answering Emilie came as a distinct and unpleasant shock. Alarm coursing through her, Addy dashed into the second-floor hallway.

At the other end of the hall, a giggling Emilie sat on the top step of the staircase, looking down. "You're not Sam, silly, Sam's my bear."

"Would he be the young fellow I saw sprawled out on the front porch?" the deep voice asked gravely.

Addy raced down the hall to where she could see part of the foyer. The man standing in the front doorway had a jacket slung over his shoulder, magazines under his arm, and carried a bulging, black briefcase with the look of expensive leather. A canvas bag sat at his feet. Faded blue jeans clung to lean hips and long legs. Addy had never seen him before. Her heart skipped a beat as he casually shut the front door with his elbow.

"You found him!" Emilie jumped to her feet and skipped down the stairs.

5

"Emilie, stop!" Addy called sharply, running to the top of the stairs. "What have I told you about talking to strangers?"

The four-year-old halted obediently and turned to look up at her aunt. "I hafta get Sam." She giggled again and pointed downward. "He says he's Sam."

Addy ignored the man. "He's a stranger, and you know you are not supposed to talk to strangers. Come back up here."

"Addy," Emilie wailed, "I want Sam."

"Upstairs. Now."

Emilie slowly, reluctantly dragged her feet up the stairs. Large, crystalline tears spilled from blue eyes to wash down pink, porcelain cheeks. She stopped in front of Addy and stamped her foot on the faded blue Oriental carpet running the length of the upstairs hallway. "Sam thinks you're mean."

"Sam doesn't like it when you talk to strangers, either," Addy said.

"Sam loves me."

Emilie didn't mean anything by her words, but the implication Addy didn't love the little girl never failed to hit a sensitive nerve. Evenly she said, "We both love you, but we don't like you doing things you know you're not supposed to do."

"Ask the man if Sam's crying. He must be very, very, very lonely." More tears cascaded down the pleading face.

Setting aside for the moment her niece's middle name ought to be Manipulation, not Adeline, Addy said, "Wash your face, and find a book to read in our sitting room. And, Emilie, stay there until I come for you. I mean it, Emilie. Stay there. I'll take care of Sam." Both Sams, she thought, steeling herself to confront the man who'd walked brazenly into the house.

Grateful for the lethally sharp blade she clutched, Addy moved slowly down the staircase, her gaze never leaving the intruder. An edgy whipcord toughness about him told her he hadn't come to sell magazines or collect for charity.

He wore his dark blond hair short and parted on the left side, a cut which suited the good bone structure of his face. The artist in her appreciated the contrasts in a lean, ascetic face which ended in a pugnacious, forward-jutting, squared-off chin. Somehow the disparate parts combined to form a devastating package of masculinity. The faintly rebellious wave in his sleek hair, a full bottom lip, and the slight droop of his left eyelid added an air of brooding sensuality. A hint of familiarity teased Addy's brain as the man watched her descend.

Her gaze met his, and the look of mixed anger and contempt in his eyes abruptly halted Addy several steps from the bottom of the staircase. The man blinked away all emotion, the blue eyes which matched his shirt turning watchful. His control frightened her more than his anger. Terrifying possibilities bombarding her mind, Addy hovered indecisively on the stairs.

"You're not quite what I'd visualized." The man studied her coolly. "The odds against a con woman having freckles must be staggering, although you might make it work—" his penetrating gaze moved slowly over her, pausing at her bare feet "—if you did away with the Gypsy-fortune teller costume and went after a wholesome, all-American, apple-pie look."

Upstairs a book fell to the floor. Emilie. Only Addy stood between the four-year-old and the stranger. Drawing herself up to look taller than her five feet, seven inches, Addy ignored the implied insult to her blue blouse and flounced green skirt and spoke with a firm self-assurance which hopefully belied her quaking insides. "We don't want whatever you're selling. If you think you can talk Mrs. Harris into giving you her life savings or any money at all, think again. Hannah might be eighty years old, but she's too savvy to be taken in by the likes of you.''

He lifted an eyebrow. ''But not the likes of you?''

She frowned at the odd remark. ''I don't know who you are, but you are tres—''

''I'm Sam Dawson. Dr. Samuel Peter Dawson.'' He barely inclined his head. ''My middle name comes from my grandfather Peter Harris. As in Peter and Hannah Harris.''

''You're one of Hannah's grandsons.'' Relief made her light-headed. No wonder he looked familiar. He starred in the framed photographs on Hannah's fireplace mantel. Ignoring the adrenaline pumping through her veins, Addy gave him an apologetic smile. ''I'm sorry, I didn't know who you were, and walking in as you did, you startled me. Hannah's not back from bridge club. You must be early. She didn't mention you were coming.''

''She didn't know. I wanted to surprise her.'' He paused half a beat. ''And you. I assume you're Adeline Johnson.''

''Surprise me?''

''I didn't want you disappearing in a puff of smoke.''

Addy frowned in puzzlement. ''Why would I disappear?''

''Disappearing before the family figures out what's going on must be the first thing crooks and charlatans learn.''

''What's going on,'' she echoed as the trend of his remarks forcibly struck her. ''You seem to be accusing me of something, Dr. Dawson. Why don't you quit hinting around and tell me exactly what I'm supposed to have done?''

His white teeth flashed. "Honesty is so disarming. I almost admire your style, Adeline."

"Ms. Johnson to you." A smile so clearly reeking of contempt should not have the power to send one's stomach dipping precipitously downward, no matter how white and even the teeth.

His eyes glittered icily as he tossed his jacket on a straight chair in the hall. "Ms. Johnson." He leaned over his briefcase, opened it and flipped through some papers. Extracting one from the middle, he handed it to her. "Read this."

The typewritten letter was addressed to Dr. Samuel Dawson. "'I saw your address on Hannah's desk, and I didn't know how to contact your mother,'" Addy read aloud, "'so I'm writing to you about something I think Hannah's family should know about. She has taken into her house a very strange woman and a child the woman claims is her niece.'" A chill crept up Addy's spine.

"Go on."

She took a deep breath and looked back down at the letter. Her hand shook slightly. "'A person reads in the newspaper about so many horrible crimes these days, and Hannah is so trusting. Hannah's husband left her a sizable trust fund and there's lots of valuable antiques in her house. I think someone in Hannah's family should investigate this woman.'" Disturbed and angry, Addy thrust the letter back at him.

"You didn't finish it."

"I don't have to. It's a bunch of garbage." As he reached for the letter, the writer's name leaped off the page at Addy. Her knees deserted her, and she sat down hard. The sharp blade slipped from nerveless fingers, falling between the staircase rails to land with a clatter on the wooden floor. She leaned against the railing, battling hurt and disbelief. How could the elderly woman she considered a friend write such spitefulness?

Addy's gaze darted around the foyer touching on the oak-paneled staircase and walls papered in blue and rose. Comforting warmth and faded gentility normally embraced her, but this man and the mean-spirited letter brought a jarring note into the familiar setting. Addy stared at the elaborate gold-framed mirror hanging over a narrow table pushed against the opposite wall. A pair of heavy silver candlesticks sat on the table, one on either side of a low silver bowl stuffed with full-blown pink and peach and yellow roses. Addy had picked those roses this morning from Cora's garden. A few fallen petals lay wilted on the polished wood. "Cora McHatton," Addy said in a hollow voice. "I can't believe Cora would... I thought she liked me."

"Cora's known my grandmother for over fifty years."

"I never had a clue she felt like that."

"Pulling off a scam must share the same success rate as drug discovery. For every winner, lots of losers. I have no idea how you schemed to fleece my grandmother, but you can consider this venture a loser, Ms. Johnson. You will remove yourself from these premises immediately."

Addy barely heard him as she sought to make sense of Cora's behavior. "I wonder if she could be growing senile. Last week she locked her keys in her car, but I didn't think anything about it. Everybody acts absent-mindedly at times."

"You're good. I should have known you would be. Grandmother isn't easily fooled."

Her head snapped up at his comments. Late afternoon sunshine streamed through the colored glass inserts over the front door, casting eerie patches of red and green and blue on his lean, uncompromising face. Addy repressed a shudder. Hannah's grandson had come halfway across the country in response to some babbling nonsense written by an elderly woman obviously suffering from senility. He'd come for one reason. To kick Addy out of the house. And Emilie. For Emilie's sake, Addy couldn't allow him to intimidate her. "You should have called Hannah. She could have told you the things Cora insinuates aren't true."

"I doubt Hannah has a clue what you're up to."

"Unlike clever you?" Addy used the stair rail to pull herself shakily to her feet. "I could have sworn Hannah said you'd earned your Ph.D., but I must have been wrong. Only idiots jump to incredibly stupid conclusions based on absolutely no evidence at all. If you'd been Albert Einstein, we'd all go around thinking rocks moved by themselves."

He frowned. "What do rocks have to do with anything?"

"You know," Addy said impatiently, moving down to the foyer. "Things not moving don't move." Detouring around him, she went out the front door and retrieved Emilie's stuffed bear from the porch. He remained rooted in the same spot when she came back inside. Ignoring his presence, she started for the stairs.

"Ms. Johnson," he said in a voice as flat as the eyes locked on her face, "you obviously believe you have ingratiated yourself into Grandmother's good graces to the extent she'll believe anything you say."

Addy willed herself not to stop and plead, not to let him see her doubts and fears. A hard-won smile of self-assurance curved her mouth. "Yes, I do, so if you thought you could fly out here and throw your weight around and I'd fall on my knees admitting guilt and begging for mercy, think again." With an exaggerated swirl of skirt, she ran lightly up the stairs.

"Ms. Johnson."

The curt summons stopped her with her hand on her sitting room doorknob. Moving to the banister, she leaned over and gave him an expectant look. "Yes? You want to apologize for calling me a crook?" His face told her nothing, but even from one floor up she sensed an unyielding toughness which promised trouble.

"I'll be staying with my grandmother for the next three weeks. You'll be gone before I leave."

Addy shoved aside the swift angry fear which flared at his threat. "It's so odd," she marveled, folding her arms on the railing and looking down with an expression of great interest. "Hannah is a bright woman, yet she claims you're brilliant. I can't imagine how you've managed to fool her all these years."

His cool upward gaze never wavered. "Sir Isaac Newton."

"What about him?"

"The laws pertaining to bodies in motion are commonly known as Newton's laws for Sir Isaac Newton, not Albert Einstein."

Addy carefully did not slam the door to her rooms. When one lived in other people's houses, one didn't slam doors. No matter how great the temptation.

"The nerve of my grandson thinking I'm an imbecile," Hannah said heatedly. Her pencil point cracked the eggshell in her hand. "Sometimes the younger generation infuriates me. Not you," she said to Addy, "but the nincompoops who think brain cells dry up once a person reaches a certain age." She looked around the large worktable at the other three ladies, who along with her constituted Addy's Wednesday morning crafts class. "Would you believe Sam thinks Addy is after my money? He not only told me so, he said he actually accused Addy to her face." She nodded her head to a chorus of "no's."

"Children," Belle Rater said indulgently, sorting through a colorful pile of ribbons and trims.

"He loves you, dear," Cora McHatton declared. "He's trying to protect you."

Sitting erect, Hannah glared at her seventy-six-year-old friend. "Who asked him to? Not me, that's for sure."

"Who wrote the letter?" Phoebe Knight asked, pausing in her paper snipping.

"I don't know." Hannah dismissed the question. "I refuse to dignify scurrilous trash by reading it." She made a face. "I suppose I should have found out who wrote it so I can give him a piece of my mind. Do you know, Addy?"

Addy shifted uneasily. She'd said nothing to Hannah about the letter, and when Hannah brought it up, Addy had assumed the older woman knew who'd written it. Addy had thought bringing the subject up while they turned eggshells into Christmas ornaments was Hannah's way of rebuking Cora without directly accusing her friend. "Why don't you ask your grandson later?"

"Because I'm asking you now," Hannah snapped. "Obviously you think I'm going to be upset by knowing the truth, but I don't appreciate my friends treating me as if I'm senile."

Her head bent, Addy concentrated on smoothing glue over her eggshell. "Cora," she muttered to the tabletop.

No one at the table suffered from hearing loss. Three pairs of outraged eyes turned to the plump, elderly widow. Affronted, Cora looked at Addy. "I didn't write Hannah's grandson any letter. Why on earth would you accuse me of such a thing, dear?"

"Sam, that is, Dr. Dawson, showed me the letter."

Cora reached across the table and patted Addy's hand. "I'm sure the letter upset you, dear, which must be why you incorrectly read the handwriting of the signature."

"It was typed." Addy wiped glue from her fingers.

"Well, there you are, dear," Cora said, "I can't type."

The other women heaped scorn and abuse on a troublemaker who'd decoyed Sam out here on a wild-goose chase, attempted to blacken Addy's reputation, and hidden behind Cora's name.

"Sam would have thrown away an anonymous letter," Phoebe said in the measured tones of one who'd been pointing out truths in a law office for half a century. "By using Cora's name, the man—or woman," she added fairly, "made the letter credible. One can only ask what purpose the letter writer had."

"You talk about your grandsons a lot," Addy said slowly to Hannah. "Maybe someone used the letter to get Dr. Dawson out here to Colorado to visit you."

"You mean I've been complaining too much about being old and useless—" Hannah waved off Addy's denial "—and someone saw himself as a Good Samaritan." She paused thoughtfully. "Someone who knew Sam prides himself on being a rational thinker. I'm not sure Sam understands about artistic expression."

The four elderly ladies turned in unison to look at Addy. Self-consciously she fingered the bright cerise, wildly patterned butterfly necklace hanging around her neck.

"Looking at you, dear, always makes me smile," Cora said.

Addy eyed her garish turquoise blouse with misgivings.

Belle, in her tiger-print jumpsuit and orange loop earrings the size of small saucers, added, "Addy is an artist. Not a calculator beside a computer attached to a test tube. Like Sam."

"Sam used to appreciate anything or anyone out of the ordinary. The oddest things would tickle his funny bone." Hannah sighed. "Once he would have been amused by the idea of someone like Addy being my roommate."

"Maybe Sam wouldn't worry so much, dear, if Addy dressed a little less colorfully..." Cora's voice trailed off.

"Nonsense," Belle boomed. "Addy is as bright and happy as her jewelry. There's no reason for her to conform to other people's narrow-minded standards."

Phoebe spoke up. "Forget about Addy's jewelry and the way she dresses. The problem is, some people think an unmarried female artist who has a child must be living a riotous life of sin and depravity."

The other elderly women nodded in somber agreement. Tired of being discussed as if she weren't present, Addy said, a tart edge to her voice, "I don't know when I'm supposed to have time to live this life of sin. Between taking care of Emilie and trying to make enough money to support us, I don't have a social life, riotous or depraved."

"Of course not," Hannah soothed, "almost everyone in town knows you're raising your sister's child."

"I set Judith Jones, over at the grocery store, straight when she called you a single mother," Belle added helpfully.

Phoebe snorted. "Judith's always been a fool."

Addy blinked away a threatening tear and smiled around the table at the four women. "I don't know what Emilie and I would do without the four of you. You are such good friends."

"Seems to me," Phoebe said, "a pretty young woman like you needs better friends than four old biddies like us."

"Don't be silly. I don't need—"

"Phoebe's right, dear," Cora interrupted. "You don't need us." Her bright determined gaze swept around the table. "What Addy needs is a husband."

Having heard Emilie's evening prayers and tucked her niece into bed with a kiss, Addy curled up in an old armchair in their sitting room. Hannah insisted Addy and Emilie consider her house their home, and they shared the bottom floor. At the same time, recognizing everyone needed some privacy, Hannah had divided the upstairs. Claiming she rattled around in the huge master bedroom with its adjoining small nursery and bathroom, Hannah had turned those rooms over to Addy and moved into the largest of the other three bedrooms. Addy and Emilie used the smaller room for their bedroom, and the former master bedroom served as a combination sitting room, playroom for Emilie, and workspace for Addy.

Leaning her head back against the chair, Addy sighed and closed her eyes. She ought to be working now. The owner of a Colorado Springs gallery had called earlier in the week to say they'd almost run out of Addy's jewelry. Addy's sales soared during the summer tourist season when she sold more of her colorful polymer clay necklaces and earrings than she did at any other time of year. The arrival in the day's mail of her bank statement with its pathetically low balance provided further incentive for buckling down to work.

She certainly had no business lolling about while Cora's absurd statement from this morning replayed itself over and over in her mind. Cora couldn't get through an hour without bemoaning the loss of her late husband Frank, so it came as no surprise to Addy the widow thought every woman needed a husband. The other three women in her Wednesday morning crafts class agreeing with Cora shocked Addy. She stirred restlessly. Even Phoebe, a confirmed spinster, maintained Addy needed a husband and Emilie needed a father.

Emilie didn't need a father. Not even the man who'd participated in her creation. Addy knew three things about him. He was rich, he was married, and he was a rotten slimy scumbag. She didn't know his name. Emilie's mother, Addy's sister Lorie, had always refused to pass on that little tidbit of information to her older sister.

Two and a half years ago Lorie had taken the name to the grave with her when she'd decided life wasn't worth living and ended hers with an overdose of sleeping pills.

Only Addy and Emilie remained, but two could make a family. Addy did not need a husband. Emilie did not need a father.

She and Emilie had everything they needed. They had a nice place to live, and Addy's income provided for them, even if they lived a somewhat hand-to-mouth existence. As long as things went smoothly... Even if things didn't go smoothly. Picking up a worn piece of wood from the small table beside her chair, Addy rubbed the familiar talisman. Johnson women survived.

The talisman failed to provide its customary strengthening reassurance. Fears and anxieties Addy had suppressed all day clawed their way to the surface. What if Hannah's grandson convinced Hannah Addy wasn't the proper companion for his grandmother? Worse, what if Sam Dawson persuaded his grandmother Addy wasn't a suitable person to be teaching arts and crafts at the community center? Addy couldn't support Emilie solely on the earnings from her jewelry sales. She clenched the worn piece of wood so tightly her hand ached. One more year, she prayed. Then Emilie would be in school most of the day, and Addy could resume teaching full-time.

She should have known this situation was too good to last. No doubt Dr. Samuel Dawson, Ph.D., had condemned Addy's character, her life-style and her clothes to Hannah. Addy had managed to avoid him since their first encounter. Mainly by keeping away from the house, since he slept down the hall and had turned the downstairs back parlor into his private office. Tonight and last night, Addy had taken Emilie out for dinner while Hannah and her grandson dined on casseroles Addy had prepared earlier and put in the freezer. Her finances didn't allow Addy to continue eating out, so she'd have to face him sooner or later. And why not? She had nothing to hide.

Someone rapped sharply from the hall. Dropping her talisman, Addy dashed to answer before the caller awakened Emilie. Hannah's grandson stood on the other side of the door.

Samuel Dawson held out her surgical blade. "You left this downstairs."

He'd come to evict them. She wouldn't make it easy for him. "Aren't you afraid I might use it on you while you're sleeping?"

"Thank you, Sam," he said. "You're welcome, Ms. Johnson."

Addy ignored the etiquette lesson. "What do you want?" She didn't invite him in, but somehow he stood in the middle of the room.

Samuel Dawson turned slowly, the vivid blue eyes not missing an inch of the crowded room. Old family photographs, Emilie's artwork, Addy's grandmother's wedding dress, vintage hats, and watercolors executed by Addy's mother hung from floor to ceiling on the rich purple walls. A tall chest and small end tables, draped with dresser scarves and tablecloths from the 1940's, held an eclectic assortment of knickknacks, framed photos, stacks of books and children's toys. More toys and stacks of books littered a floor spread with assorted fragments of Oriental-style carpets and scattered with heaps of huge bright pillows. A green paisley print bedsheet covered the sagging sofa, while the two old armchairs sported green, red and purple stripes. Addy's craft tools and Emilie's art projects filled every spare inch of the old painted dining room table and spilled over onto the floor. Addy's storage system, boxes of all sizes and shapes, wrapped in decorative papers, wallpaper and fabric, took up what little space remained on the floor, on the tables, and on the chest. A multitude of potted plants lined the windowsills across the front of the house.

Addy hoped Samuel Dawson's raised eyebrows didn't fly right off the top of his head.

"This room must violate every fire code known to man."

"No, it doesn't, and before you get the brilliant idea of reporting me to the fire department in hopes Hannah will be forced to evict me, you ought to know the fire chief's son is in my puppet-making class and her daughter is in Emilie's play group." He didn't need to know, if she wasn't barefoot, Addy'd be quaking in her shoes. The barest lift of one of his eyebrows could be interpreted as his acknowledgment of her firm position. Or he could be mocking her for being so stupid she didn't know the treacherous insecurity of her position. Addy clenched her hands at her side. She knew.

Sam Dawson picked up a framed snapshot of an ethereal blond beauty holding a cherubic, blue-eyed baby and minutely scrutinized the photo. "Your niece and her mother?"

"Yes."

"You don't look much like your sister."

Addy carefully set the surgical blade on the nearest table. If she held on to it, she'd be tempted to use it on him. She snatched the photograph from his grasp and polished his fingerprints from the glass and frame with her caftan before returning the picture to its resting place. She wouldn't let him intimidate her. Battles needed to be fought head-on. "She took after my mother's side of the family. I took after my dad's." Practically seeing the words, "How unfortunate," forming on his lips, she hastily inquired in acid tones what else he wanted in a none-too-subtle hint he be on his way.

He moved further into the room. Stopping in front of one of her mother's paintings, he studied the haphazard splotches of color and leaned closer to peer at the signature. "Lily Johnson. Your sister?"

"No."

The clipped denial turned up one corner of his mouth an infinitesimal amount. "Just someone who couldn't paint her way out of a paper bag and who coincidentally shares your last name?"

"My mother painted the picture you're sneering at."

"Why didn't you say so in the first place?"

"My room, my paintings, my sister, my mother and anything and everything else about my life are none of your business."

Her proclamation bounced heedlessly off him. "You're worse than a damned pack rat. A psychiatrist would have a field day with this messy room and what it says about how insecure you are. Or what a control freak you are."

"I'm not insecure or a control freak, and this room is not messy. It's lived in."

"It's cluttered, chaotic, gaudy, and an assault to the nervous system. Why don't you get rid of some of this junk?"

"I'd love to. Starting with you."

Stepping over a ball, some crayons and an abandoned baby doll, he seated himself in one of the armchairs and pointed to the other. "Sit down. I want to talk to you."

Addy considered refusing, but he'd obviously prepared a speech, and just as obviously she wasn't going to get rid of him until he'd had his say. Ignoring the chair he'd pointed to, she moved Emilie's play clay to one side and sat down on the sofa, tucking her legs beneath her.

"Cora did not write the letter to me," he said.

"There's a news flash."

He gazed levelly at her. "Grandmother is satisfied you are whom you say you are."

"But you're not."

"I'll wait for more data before I make up my mind. Grandmother, however, not only believes you, she's worried about you. Anyone out to get you, Ms. Johnson?"

"Unlike you, I don't go around offending people."

He engaged in deliberate, protracted study of her electric teal blue caftan before raising mocking eyes to her face. "That's difficult to believe."

Addy jumped to her feet. So much for patiently hearing what he had to say. "There's no reason for Hannah to be worried about me, so good night, Dr. Dawson."

He stretched his legs out in front of him and leaned back in the chair. "Grandmother wants me to keep an eye on you for the next couple of weeks, for your protection."

"I don't want you anywhere near me, and I don't need any protection. There is absolutely no reason for Hannah to worry about me. Some busybody doubtlessly thought it time someone in Hannah's family bothered to visit her, and I got the dubious honor of being the carrot. Or maybe the stick."

His face darkened and he asked in a chilly voice, "Are you accusing my family of neglecting Grandmother?"

Addy wasn't about to back down. "I've known Hannah for over nine months, and not once has a member of her family visited her, and not once has she gone to visit any of them. Emilie and I and Phoebe spent Christmas Day with her. We—" she emphasized the word "—had nowhere else to go and no one else to spend the holiday with." For a moment Addy thought she glimpsed a slight hint of mortification color his cheeks. The next second she knew she'd imagined it.

"My parents opened in a play in Florida, and Grandmother no longer enjoys the hustle and bustle of backstage. As for my brothers, Harry was in Africa, and Mike had to work the hospital emergency room Christmas Day.'' He added evenly, ''I was involved in complicated negotiations raising venture capital for a small start-up company in California.''

''Such busy, busy lives,'' Addy mocked. ''Hannah's eighty years old. Will you all be too busy to come to her funeral?''

Sam Dawson's eyes narrowed to dark blue slits, and he stared at her for the longest moment. ''You did it,'' he said slowly. ''You wrote the letter.''

CHAPTER TWO

HIS absurd conclusion rendered Addy speechless. Almost. "You're crazy. Absolutely, positively, certifiably crazy. What possible reason could I have for writing such a letter?"

"To convince me you're nothing more than a meddling, busybody, who arbitrarily decided Grandmother's family neglected her, so you mailed off a letter expressly designed to compel at least one of her family to rush to her rescue."

"Offering myself up as some kind of sacrificial lamb?" she asked sarcastically.

"I can't imagine anyone less lamblike." He studied her thoughtfully, his elbows and hands resting on the arms of the large striped armchair. "You're more clever than I first realized. I'm sure Grandmother's welfare was the furthest thing from your mind. What happened? Were others around town beginning to question why Grandmother suddenly took in a strange young woman and her child? Writing me the letter would be a brilliant maneuver on your part. I'd come out, see you and Emilie living innocently upstairs, pronounce you harmless, and go home." He paused. "You'd be free to manipulate and swindle Grandmother out of her last penny, secure in the knowledge I'd ignore any further warnings emanating from here."

"I should be grateful, if I'm to be called a crook, at least I'm clever and brilliant. Which is more than I can say about you. I keep looking for a glimmer of this brilliance Hannah brags you have, but you hide it well.

Phoebe thinks Judith Jones is a fool. I'd hate to hear what she thinks about you."

"Phoebe Knight? Is she to be your next victim?"

Addy wanted to grind her molars. Preferably with his stupid, single-minded head between them. "Phoebe spent almost fifty years working as a secretary for a law firm. I'll bet she involved herself in all kinds of graft and blackmail and embezzlement." Only a tiny quiver in her voice betrayed Addy's amusement at the improbable thought of Phoebe so much as jay-walking. "Who knows how much dough she has stashed away? Of course, I'd have to be either terribly brilliant or terribly stupid to think I could bamboozle Phoebe." Inwardly conceding Sam Dawson would leave when he wanted to leave and not a second sooner, Addy again lowered herself to the sofa. "One would think I'd victimize Cora McHatton or Belle Rater."

"Although Belle made out like a bandit when she sold the family hotel to that large hotel chain, I seem to recall a daughter who's an attorney in Denver. I imagine it didn't take you long to ferret out the fact that, although Cora is comfortable, she's not as wealthy as some people think she is. Her husband was notorious for accepting chickens and garden produce and amateurish art-work—" he barely glanced at one of Lily's paintings "—instead of billing his poorer patients."

Believing the doctor's widow to be rolling in dough, Addy occasionally found Cora's little economies irri-tating. She resolved to be more patient and under-standing. With Cora. Addy had no patience for unwanted visitors. "If you don't quit overworking your puny little brain, inventing criminally convoluted reasons for my living here, you're going to strain it. You'd better run back to Boston before you give yourself a migraine."

"You're the one who'll be running, not me." The threat held no less menace for being delivered in a conversational voice.

Addy swallowed. "I'm not going anywhere. Hannah trusts me."

His lazy smile held no warmth. "If it comes to her having to make a choice between us, whom do you think she'll choose? Adeline, you'll be out of here by the end of the week."

"Don't call me Adeline." His smile annoyed her. She wondered who'd told him he should always wear blue shirts the color of his eyes.

"The end of the week, Ms. Johnson." He took his time looking around the room before his steel-forged gaze returned to her. "With all this junk, you'd better start packing. Anything you leave behind, I'll donate to the nearest thrift shop."

Addy grabbed a scarlet pillow, squashing it against her middle. "I'm not leaving anything behind, because I'm not going anywhere. My living arrangements are between me and Hannah, and have nothing to do with you."

"I won't even ask you to repaint these outlandish purple walls, and I'll refund any rent money owing."

"There is no rent money owing."

"You don't pay rent monthly from the first of the month?"

"I don't pay rent at all." The slightest tensing of Sam Dawson's muscles told Addy that Hannah had neglected to mention a few minor details to her grandson.

"I'd be interested," he said slowly, "in hearing exactly how that set of circumstances transpired."

He'd accused her of everything from meddling to chicanery. This from the man who could have earned his Ph.D. in arbitrarily meddling in other people's lives. Somebody needed to explain to Samuel Dawson, Ph.D., no one had appointed him Grand Poohbah, charged with making other people's decisions for them based on what he thought best. Addy gripped the rumpled pillow and looked squarely at him. "The idea came from you."

"I doubt that."

"You hired Mary to live with your grandmother. Mary's whole life centered on TV soap operas. Hannah about went crazy."

"I bought Mary a television set for her room," he said.

"Half the pleasure in the soaps for Mary was discussing them. What did Hannah think this husband or that wife or that lover was going to do, et cetera and so on. Fortunately she decided her daughter needed her and moved to Durango."

"Ninna didn't watch soaps."

"Ninna thought anyone as old as Hannah must be decrepit, blind, deaf and feeble-minded. She shouted to your grandmother, patronized her and fussed over her until Hannah wanted to strangle her."

"Grandmother deserves a little cosseting," he said.

"Cosseting?" His closed face and cool voice gave little away, but Addy recognized defensive squirming when she heard it. "Bells on Hannah's doorknob so Ninna would hear Hannah get up. Opening Hannah's mail and reading it out loud to her to make sure she understood it. Not allowing Hannah to take her daily walk if it rained, or the wind blew, or the day was too hot or too cold."

"I terminated Ninna's employment," he said tightly.

"Because she annoyed you, phoning you all the time to tattle on Hannah. You immediately replaced her with Ethel."

"What was wrong with Ethel?" he challenged. "She was a charming, friendly, middle-aged woman who—"

"Talked. And talked. And talked. Non-stop. About nothing." Addy shuddered dramatically. "I only know by reputation of the other ladies you hired to live with your grandmother, but Ethel came to my crafts classes with Hannah."

"Grandmother never complained to me about Ethel. I didn't even know she'd let her go until I arrived here."

"Let her go?" Addy asked derisively. "As if Hannah would fire anyone you hired. She married off Ethel to Pete Browne who liked her cooking. Hannah said he could turn off his hearing aid."

"If you're accusing me of forcing my grandmother to share her home with incompatible companions..." He paused before continuing in a measured voice, "Grandmother had only to say the woman wasn't acceptable to her."

"The way she told you she didn't need, and didn't want, a companion living with her?"

"Grandmother is eighty years old." Two balls of blue ice stared coldly at Addy. "I did not," he said, spacing out the words, "force her to hire a companion. I merely suggested the family would feel more comfortable if she did."

Clearly, Sam Dawson thought Sam Dawson knew best. Addy nodded her head. "Emotional blackmail is the most effective."

He rose abruptly to his feet. "You have two days to vacate these premises. Start packing."

He erred in thinking her easily bullied. Slowly she stood up. "Please leave this room." Her hands turned into tight fists at her sides. "It's mine and you're not welcome in it."

"You may be able to force my grandmother out of her own bedroom, but I'm not a feeble, eighty-year-old woman. I want you out of this house in two days."

No hint of anger warmed his cold, implacable voice. Long practice must enable him to control his facial muscles and emotions so completely. A concrete wall had more give to it. Addy fought the weariness invading her muscles. Years of being shunted from one relative to another should have taught her the dangers of viewing someone else's home as hers. A despairing lump swelled in Addy's throat. Emilie knew happiness here with her new friends and borrowed family. Addy straightened her shoulders. "Hannah and I have a legally-binding agreement, even if it's not written down. You need a court order to evict me." She didn't have the faintest idea if what she said was valid.

The sardonic smile on Sam Dawson's face mocked her defiance. "Mary wasn't the only one watching too much television."

"If you want me out, you're going to have to physically remove me."

"Fine." Hands on his hips, he swiftly surveyed his immediate surroundings. "I'll start with this." He snatched an item from the nearest table. Striding across the room, he opened the window to the upper porch and hurled the small object into the night.

Guessing his intention too late to stop him, Addy stood transfixed for the barest fraction of a second, then she whirled and dashed from the room, tearing down the staircase and through the front door, heedless of the impatient voice and thunderous footsteps behind her. Falling to her knees, she groped blindly in the dark, frantically patting her hands on the ground around her. She encountered nothing but prickly grass.

"Get up. You won't find it in the dark." Hard fingers dug into her shoulders and hauled her to her feet. "Damn it, you could have broken a leg or something running down the staircase. Are you crazy?"

"Let go of me." She needed a flashlight. Breaking free of his hold, she ran into the house. In the bedroom she hunted quickly and silently for the flashlight, freezing in place when Emilie stirred briefly in her sleep. Finding the flashlight, Addy slipped from the bedroom, carefully closing the door behind her. The battery was dead. Addy slumped against the door, the cold, useless metal flashlight clutched in one hand. Her eyes shut, she endeavored to catch her breath.

"What the hell was that all about?"

Addy's eyes popped open at the harsh voice unexpectedly close to her. He must be at least six feet tall, she thought stupidly. She wore no shoes, but he easily topped her height. His stance radiated hostility, with his fists jammed on his hips and his jeans-clad legs spread wide. A frown lowered his eyebrows. She hated him. A bubble of hysteria stuck in her throat. Hated him and his blue shirts which matched his eyes. "Get out."

His frown darkened. "I'm not going anywhere until you tell me why you went tearing outside after a stick."

"Get out of here or I'm going to call the police and charge you with—" She groped for the right word, "—vandalism."

"For throwing an old stick out the window?" Equal parts irritation and bewilderment colored his voice.

A hot rush of moisture threatened, and Addy determinedly blinked it away. Tears had never been her weapon nor her refuge. "It was not an old stick. It was a clothespin."

"You went berserk over a clothespin?"

"When my great-grandmother's house burned down, all she managed to save was herself, her cat, and a few clothespins outside on the clothesline." Addy's great-grandmother had been a fifty-six-year-old widow who'd seen her life's work and memories reduced to ashes. Instead of giving up and moving in with one of her kids, she'd cooked and cleaned, bartering her services for carpenter work until she'd replaced the burnt embers with a tiny one-room house. "That clothespin—" Addy swallowed hard "—isn't just a clothespin." He'd thrown her lucky piece, her hope, her strength out the window.

The old, yellowed lace curtains swayed in the slight breeze coming through her opened window. The engine of a passing car labored as it made its way up the steep road in front of the house. A hint of exhaust drifted inside.

Sam Dawson stirred. "I assumed it was a stick your little girl had carried in. I'll find it in the morning." He paused. "If an old clothespin belonging to your great-grandmother means so much to you, you should understand why I feel compelled to do what's best for Grandmother."

"What you think is best for her isn't necessarily what's best for her."

"I've known my grandmother for thirty-five years. I think I'm a better judge of her needs than a stranger is. Even if you aren't a con woman, she doesn't need the stress of turning over part of her home to a rambunctious child and a woman like you."

"A woman like me?" Addy asked tightly.

His quick glance encompassed the room. "You're not exactly a restful person. Everything about you, this room, the way you dress, your life-style—"

"You know nothing about me or my life-style."

He gazed thoughtfully at her. "You have the most expressive face I've ever seen. Actresses would love to know how you manage to convey so much information and emotion in a single look." A slight smile curved his mouth. "Like now. You're mad and surprised." His eyes narrowed. "And frightened." He took a step closer. "Do I scare you, Adeline? Or are you hiding something you're afraid I'll find out?"

"I'm not afraid of you or anything else," she lied. He stood too close to her.

"I wonder if any scientific studies have been done on whether a woman with freckles—" he trailed a finger among hers "—is more or less complicated than an unfreckled woman. Your eyes are more gray than blue." He ran his thumb along the top of her cheekbone under her eye. "They tell me you're scared, but defiant." He wrapped his hands around her face. "And interested."

The husky timbre of his voice pulsated through her body. "I'm not," she managed to say. Her stomach engaged in death-defying gyrations as her gaze collided with a smoldering one. Any urge to kiss him was hopelessly juvenile. Sam Dawson might posses dark blond good looks, Paul Newman eyes, and a sleek and sexy masculine physique, but he had all the warmth of a fiberglass sport car. He was a coldhearted, overbearing automation with steel-clad control.

And warm lips.

For the first time Addy understood what her sister Lorie had meant about how a woman could be attracted to the wrong man. Yielding to the gentle pressure of Sam's mouth, Addy parted her lips. Her hands curled into fists against his smooth, cool shirtfront. Cool for only a second and then the heat from his skin penetrated the silky fabric.

He lifted his head. "It's those damned freckles. They trick a man into forgetting how dangerous you are."

"Dangerous?" She outlined his chin with her finger. A man possessing such a firm, square chin laughed at danger. Unseen whiskers rasped against her skin. The tip of her finger burned where it touched his skin. She moved her finger to his lips. Lips should be cooler. His weren't.

He captured her finger, his large, warm hand curling around it. "Give it up."

"Give up what?" His mouth inches away mesmerized her.

"Trying to seduce me into changing my mind. I'm not excited by women who use sex as a bargaining chip."

The harsh words belatedly dispelled the dazed fog blanketing Addy's brain. "You kissed me." Sam Dawson held her loosely against him; her fingers splayed against his warm chest. Summoning every bit of self-control she'd ever hoped to possess, she removed his hands and stepped away. "I have no intention of bargaining." Her legs might be wobbling beneath her floor-length caftan, but her calm, cool voice did her proud. "It's clear you don't listen to common sense or your grandmother, but are guided solely by your ego, and knowing where so many men's egos are located..." She shrugged. "If a couple of kisses would get you out of your grandmother's hair, it seemed petty of me not to oblige. You're the one who claims Hannah shouldn't be stressed."

"I'm also the one giving you two days to make other living arrangements. And, Adeline, if, instead of packing, you want to spend those two days trying to make me change my mind..." Cool amusement threaded through his voice. "Go ahead. I might not be adverse to seeing if your—shall we say, theatrical life-style?—extends to other areas besides clothing and interior decoration."

"What a shame my standards," Addy said immediately, "don't sink that low." She took a deep breath. "Whether I move or not is up to Hannah, but since we do agree these are my rooms, at least for the next two days, I want you to get out and stay out." She walked away, throwing words of exaggerated politeness over her shoulder. "If you will please excuse me, I need to wash your germs off my face."

Shutting the bathroom door behind her, Addy gripped the edge of the old porcelain sink, wishing her fingers gripped Samuel Dawson's neck. Of all the conceited, egotistical, arrogant jerks... She grabbed a washcloth to scrub her face. To scrub away his kisses. And caught sight of herself in the mirror. Addy didn't remember him untying the ribbon at the end of her braid, but her brown hair hung in loose array around her shoulders. She brushed it back, and the metal fittings on the emerald green fish dangling from her ears glinted in the harsh overhead light. Her freckles stood out against her pale skin, her wide-set eyes were circles of grayish blue.

If she'd been wearing lip color when he arrived, her mouth was wiped clean now. She ran a finger over her bottom lip. Her lips looked normal. She only imagined her mouth was swollen and bruised. Regardless of his prejudice against her, his kisses had been gentle. And devastating. No, she wouldn't think about that. If it hadn't been so long since she'd been kissed by a man, she'd remember other kisses had been wonderful. Sam Dawson didn't hold the monopoly on earth-shaking kisses.

She shook a finger at the slightly bemused eyes in the mirror. "You are acting like a lovesick, love-starved adolescent, Addy Johnson." Acting. She turned on the cold water, allowing a quiet trickle to dampen the facecloth. Sam Dawson's mother and father acted on the stage. Hannah said if Sam's interests hadn't steered him elsewhere, he'd have been an Academy Award winning actor.

He'd been acting. He hadn't meant a single one of his kisses. He'd been trying to breach her defenses because he wanted her out of his grandmother's house. He was such a conceited, egotistical, arrogant jerk, he believed she'd sleep with him on her way out the door.

Out the door. Weakness washed over her, and she leaned over the cold sink, supported by her outstretched arms. Hannah enjoyed having Addy and Emilie in her home, but was her enjoyment strong enough to counter the strong-willed wishes of her grandson? Hannah claimed she loved her three grandsons equally, but Addy had heard enough stories to know Sam was favored. Addy hated to think what Hannah's other two grandsons were like. Not that it mattered. They weren't here in Colorado determined to uproot Addy and Emilie. Samuel Dawson was.

Her mind reviewed every tidbit about him Hannah had dropped. He'd earned his Ph.D. in Chemistry before he reached thirty. Given a choice between working for a major drug company and helping a former university professor start up a biotech company, he'd chosen the latter. The rapid realization, that as businessmen, the scientists were neophytes, sent him careening off in a new career direction. Sam's research hours had dwindled while he studied intensively for an M.B.A., racing to gather enough business knowledge to advise and assist his former professor.

Two years ago, diagnosed with prostate cancer, the professor sold his company and retired. Declining to accept the attractive offer made him by the new company officers, Sam had cashed his options and set up his own business, offering himself as a consultant to other biotech firms. His financial acumen combined with his doctorate in chemistry made him extremely attractive to the myriad small biotech firms springing up worldwide.

Hannah had shown Addy a business magazine article dubbing Sam an instant success. He wasn't, of course. Addy turned off the water with a forceful twist, painfully jamming her palm. Hard work, determination and single-mindedness had gotten him where he was. Traits not likely to work in Addy's favor.

Two photos hung beside the mirror. Baby portraits of Lorie and Emilie taken over twenty years apart. "I'll fight," Addy said quietly. "You know I'll do anything

for Emilie. If I have to beg Hannah to let us stay, I will."
As for Dr. Samuel Dawson, Ph.D., she didn't plan to
talk to him ever again.

Sam Dawson sat on the sofa in the sitting room, Emilie
curled in his lap. The little girl wore an old T-shirt which
had been washed so often only memory told Addy it
originally had been bright pink. The neck binding had
been replaced more than once and gay patches covered
stains and holes, but the neck slipped off Emilie's
shoulders and new spots and holes needed to be cam-
ouflaged. Emilie's chubby little bare feet pressed against
the sofa arm as she giggled at something Sam said. She
looked like a ragged, tattered waif.

Addy inhaled sharply. "What are you doing out of
bed, young lady?"

"Addy," Emilie said delightedly, "Sam was children
here. He stayed with his grandma when he was little like
me."

"His name is Dr. Dawson," Addy corrected.

Emilie stubbornly shook her head. "Sam." Straight-
ening up, she bestowed one of her beatific smiles on him
and said, "You hafta be Sam man, cuz he's—" she held
up her stuffed toy "—Sam bear." She snuggled up
against Sam's chest. His arms seemed to curve instinctively around the small body.

Pain sliced through Addy's chest. This wasn't the first
time Emilie had reached out to a man, any man. Emilie
was too young to know monsters sometimes wore
friendly smiles, so she snuggled up to the man who smiled
at her even as he intended to evict them. Pain turned to
anger at Sam Dawson's hypocrisy, and Addy spoke
curtly. "Emilie, you are supposed to be in bed. March
right back there."

"Sam take me," Emilie demanded.

Before Addy could refuse, he stood up, Emilie secure in his arms. "Your carriage awaits, Your Highness. Point the way to your bedroom."

Emilie giggled. "You're silly. I like you."

The pain intensified. The ability to captivate every male in sight between the ages of two and two hundred had brought Lorie nothing but grief. Addy worried Emilie was her mother's daughter. Unbelievably, the blue-eyed, towheaded, almost-five-years-old little girl had melted cold eyes and softened a lean, hard face and pugnacious, square chin. Addy didn't believe it. He was acting again.

Addy pulled back the covers on the twin-size bed, and Sam Dawson laid Emilie down, placing her bear beside her. Addy straightened the covers over her niece and bent to kiss Emilie's soft cheek. Lifting her head she fixed a mock scowl on her face. "I don't want to see you again until morning."

Emilie threw her arms around Addy's neck and pulled her closer. "Addy maddy?" she asked.

They'd long played this game. "Well..." Addy drew out the word.

"No," Emilie shouted. "Addy not maddy 'cuz I love you." She aimed a loud, smacking kiss at Addy's cheek.

Addy gave her a little squeeze. "I love you, too, you little pumpkin head. Now go to sleep."

"Kiss first," Emilie ordered bossily.

"I already kissed you," Addy said.

"Not you." Emilie removed her arms from Addy's neck and held them up. "Sam man kiss."

Addy turned her back and concentrated on swallowing the painfully huge lump in her throat. Emilie was merely postponing her bedtime. She didn't need a man in her life. She certainly didn't need a hard, immovable, two-faced, egotistical stranger.

Sam followed her from the room. "Cute kid."

"I think so. Good night." Her back to him, she prayed he'd leave without further discussion. If the world she'd carefully constructed to protect Emilie seemed pitifully frail at this precise moment, blame it on her tiredness. And Sam Dawson. Addy's life had been excellent training for taking setbacks in stride, but suddenly, not for a million dollars could she summon up one iota of optimism and hope for her and Emilie's future. She should pack up and move. There were other apartments. Other jobs. No. She liked living with Hannah. She liked teaching at the community center. Taking a deep breath, she firmed up her spine. Life was not going to exhaust and drain and beat her down. Not life, and not Samuel Dawson.

"You ought to sell some of this junk in here and buy the poor kid a pair of decent pajamas," he said.

"She has plenty of pajamas." Addy spun around. "OK, so I bought them at a thrift store, but they looked brand new. She insists on sleeping in that T-shirt because her mother used to wear it. She doesn't even remember Lorie. Emilie knows nothing of her mother but some pictures, that T-shirt and Lorie's old stuffed bear." One stupid tear came from nowhere to burn her cheek. "You think that's the same as having a mother?"

"Her father—"

"She has no father. Her mother signed papers. In exchange for a huge chunk of money, my sister promised to never divulge her lover's name or ask him for more money." The minute the words left her mouth, Addy wished she could recall them. She normally avoided discussing her situation, but this man had her so discombobulated, she'd come dangerously close to succumbing to self-pity in front of him. More reason to intensely dislike him.

"Not too huge a chunk of money," he said, "not if you have to shop in thrift shops and live in rooms in an elderly woman's house. Or else you had a good time while it lasted.''

The fact Lorie had blown the money out in California before committing suicide was none of his business. Addy thrust out her chin. "I had a really good time. Steak and champagne. Penthouse apartments. You might be seeing me down on my luck, but I expect to have plenty of money rolling in soon."

"Planning to win the Colorado lottery?"

"Same as." She sniffed and crossed her arms across her chest. "Have you forgotten my scam to fleece Hannah and her senile friends?"

He contemplated her. "Data can be tricky. There has to be enough, and one must be careful interpreting it. The woman I thought you were wouldn't have taken on the responsibility of raising someone else's child." He took a step toward her.

"Don't be naive. Emilie is my biggest asset. One minute with her and suckers' brains turn to mush."

"You can't be a successful confidence woman," he said. "Divulging your methods and putting me on guard."

"To the contrary, I'm brilliant. I've been so engagingly candid with you, you're now convinced I'm perfectly harmless."

He stood in front of her and curved his hand around her cheek. "I doubt you're perfectly harmless."

Anger and another emotion, one less easily categorized, simmered in her veins. "If I'm dangerous, you'd better run back to your safe little Boston cubbyhole before I fleece you."

"I'm not worried." He brushed back her hair and scrutinized her face. "Who are you, Adeline Johnson? The wild clothes and the purple walls say one thing. The old clothespin and this junk say something different. Then there's the woman who shops in thrift stores and keeps patching an ancient T-shirt out of love. Which are you?''

She pushed his hand away from her face. ''I thought the brilliant Dr. Dawson had all the answers.''

''There are too many questions for anyone to have all the answers. One of the reasons I've always been intrigued by puzzles. You, Adeline, definitely puzzle me.''

''You're as easy to hoodwink as your grandmother is.''

''Grandmother isn't the least bit easy to hoodwink.''

''Maybe when she was younger and still had brains,'' Addy said sarcastically, ''but everyone knows when a person turns sixty she becomes senile and loses all judgment.''

''You think I'm insufferably arrogant, don't you?''
''Yes.''

He moved to another subject. ''Grandmother told me about the play group you organized at the center. Mainly so Emilie could attend, she thought. I think I see a pattern here. You've built your life around Emilie.'' He stopped a moment, then said deliberately, ''Emilie calls my grandmother, Grandma Hannah.''

''You'd prefer Mrs. Harris?''

''You moved in here to give Emilie a grandmother.''

''Don't be silly. The landlord of my last apartment raised the rent to an outrageous sum which I couldn't afford. Hannah knew if she didn't move a companion of her choice in here, you'd shove another witless wonder on her. Hannah isn't our family. She's my employer. I live here, do the shopping and cook dinner, and we manage to keep out of each other's way.''

''Grandmother said she and Emilie frequently nap together. Don't bother to deny it. I've seen the children's books in Grandmother's bedroom, Emilie's chair in the front parlor and the crayons in the silver tray in the dining room.''

"So?" Addy challenged.

"Living here must be inconvenient for you, not to mention a drag on your social life."

"My social life is just fine, thank you very much."

He held her upper arms when she would have turned away. "When did you last have a date?"

"What's it to you, Dr. Drive-his-mother-and-grandmother-crazy because he never gives the beautiful women his mother regularly trots past him a second look."

He stared down at her, an arrested look in his blue eyes. "I'll be damned." A humorless grin slashed across his face, and his fingers tightened around her arms. "You and my mother and my grandmother. The three of you came up with that letter."

Addy heaved a heavy sigh. "Next you'll accuse the entire population of Ute Pass of being in some kind of conspiracy. The purpose of which totally defeats me."

"Does it? Try marriage. Me to you. I've heard that complaint you just parroted about my single state from Mom's and Grandmother's lips more times than I care to think about. They've been scheming to marry me off since I turned thirty."

"That's your problem, not mine."

"With that letter you became my problem. Obviously the matchmaking met with your approval. Raising a kid on your own, struggling to pay the bills... Marriage to someone like me must have seemed the answer to your prayers."

"Of all the idiotic, conceited..." Addy jerked out of his grasp. "You've spent too much time in the laboratory. Something mutated and ate your brain."

"Convince me I'm wrong."

"Even if I cared to try, which I don't, trying to convince a pig-headed ignoramus of anything is a total waste of time. You've made up your mind and no facts are going to sway you."

"You want to talk facts? Fine. Fact number one. Whoever wrote the letter knew it would bring me on the run."

"How about the fact I think you're a blistering pain in the neck?" She may as well have saved her breath.

"Fact number two. Emilie needs a father."

"No, she doesn't."

"Fact number three," Sam continued relentlessly. "Emilie is your life. Which means you'd do anything for her, including marrying to provide her with a father."

"She doesn't need a father."

"Grandmother made a point of telling me she and her friends offered to find you a husband, but she said you have a prospective mate in mind. That's a lie, isn't it?" He went on without waiting for her answer. "Was it Grandmother's idea, my mother's or yours that you play hard to get?"

Addy flapped her mouth open and shut like a trout. When the ladies had approached the subject of her needing a husband, Addy had hinted at a boyfriend. Stammering, she tried to explain. "Not Hannah's idea. I mean, they did mention they knew some available men. They suggested fixing me up. I thought if they thought— I saw how they dispatched Ethel, and the idea of their persistent matchmaking turning in my direction... You don't know... Those women, once they decide a woman needs to be married, are tireless and creative. I saw myself herded down the aisle and..." Her explanation ground to a halt at the pronounced skepticism on his face. "If you'd seen them intent on marrying off Ethel," she said mulishly, "you wouldn't be giving me that look."

He shook his head. "A word to the wise, Ms. Johnson. Regardless of what she says, my mother is not privy to my social life. I have all the dates I want, and when I marry, the bride will be one I select, not one chosen by my female relatives. And she sure as hell won't be a freckle-faced, wildly-dressed Gypsy with a ready-made family. No offense," he added offensively.

"I may have freckles," Addy retorted, "but at least I'm human, which is more than can be said for you. Even your own grandmother claims you have dry ice in your veins."

"Not dry ice."

"What?" She practically screeched the word.

"Dry ice is a solid. Carbon dioxide. It vaporizes without liquefying."

"You think I care?" She definitely screeched.

"One should always care about accuracy."

The rational response delivered in a reasonable tone of voice snapped what little restraint Addy had left. She shoved him out into the hall and slammed her door. Prepared to throw her body against the solid wood if he tried to return, she welcomed the sound of his footsteps moving away.

The sinking feeling deep in the pit of her stomach stayed with her. Sam's recitation of facts revealed the awful truth to Addy. "Hannah, Hannah. Whatever could you have been thinking?"

CHAPTER THREE

"I DON'T know, Addy," Hannah said Thursday morning. "It seemed like a good idea at the time."

"Hannah Harris! You must be getting senile in your old age," Belle said indignantly.

"The very idea," Phoebe added in outrage, "writing a warning letter to your own grandson to lure him out here."

"I thought," Hannah said, remorse absolutely dripping from her tongue, "Sam and Addy would make the perfect couple."

Addy had brought Emilie for her story hour at the community center and seen the four women chatting while they decorated more Christmas eggs. Seeing no one else in the crafts room, Addy had taken advantage of the opportunity to confront Hannah without Sam or Emilie being present. Standing at one end of the long table, Addy looked severely at the four elderly women. "There's no point in any of you acting innocent. I know you were all in cahoots. I haven't forgotten the lengths you four went to when you railroaded poor Pete and Ethel into marriage."

"They're very happy, dear," Cora said complacently. "I think Pete's put on weight since they married. I always said Ethel's a wonderful cook. Not that you aren't a good cook, dear." She glanced up from under her impossibly blond hair, then quickly returned her attention to the egg she rolled in glitter. "Hannah says Sam is a good eater."

43

"I'm not the least bit interested in Sam's eating habits."

"More's the shame, dear. He's so good-looking. And money wouldn't be a problem for you anymore."

"Call me old-fashioned, but I prefer to marry for love," Addy said tartly.

"My daddy always said it's as easy to fall in love with a rich man as a poor one," Belle said.

"We're sorry, Addy," Phoebe added. "We made a mistake with the letter. We've all known Sam since he was a baby, and maybe it's a little difficult for us to view him objectively. We should have realized you are unsuited for each other."

Emilie could have told them Dr. Samuel Dawson, Ph.D., and Adeline Johnson would go together like fingerpaints and white party dresses, Addy thought morosely. Guilt flooded her at the sight of Hannah sitting silently, staring at the table. Addy hadn't intended to hurt the elderly woman's feelings. "It's not that your grandson's not nice, Hannah. I'm sure he's perfectly charming," she lied, "but he and I simply aren't compatible."

"You're right. We'll drop the whole thing," Hannah said.

"Yes," Belle agreed, "let's just forget about it, and Hannah can enjoy Sam's visit. I saw him at the post office this morning. He gets handsomer every time I see him. And so polite. Addy, I love your red and fuchsia cat and dog necklace with that purple blouse. You have a wonderful sense of color. What color trim do you think I should put with this violet angel?"

Addy glared around the table. "That's it? You write a stupid letter, cause me no end of trouble, and all you have to say is it seemed like a good idea, let's forget about it, and what goes with violet? May I remind you

Dr. Dawson thinks I had something to do with writing that letter?"

"Sticks and stones, dear."

Before Addy could leap across the table and strangle Cora with her own wig, Belle said quickly, "It's not as if it matters to you what Sam thinks. Does it, Addy?"

"Of course not." So why was she making an issue of it?

"You haven't committed any crime, and there's nothing he can do to you," Phoebe added.

"He ordered me to move."

"It's Hannah's house," Phoebe said. "Ignore him."

"It's not pleasant being accused of luring him out here so I can trap him into marriage. And it's pretty difficult to avoid someone who's living in the same house."

"You need a man, dear."

"Cora, I swear, if you tell me one more time—"

"Now, Addy, Cora's right," Belle interrupted. "If Sam saw you dating other men, he'd know his suspicions were entirely wrong, and the whole matter would swiftly die away."

Their entire diabolical scheme burst full-blown in Addy's head. In grand and glorious primary colors. She collapsed on the metal chair behind her. "You're unbelievable," she breathed. "If Machiavelli were alive today, he'd worship at your feet. For the past several months the four of you have wanted to match me up with one man or another, but I put you off, so you wrote Hannah's grandson, forcing him to drop everything and rush out here. He's a red herring, isn't he? While he annoyed and distracted me, you planned to marry me off to someone else before I realized what was happening. I find it hard to believe Dr. Dawson's in on your scheme, which means he's going to kill you, and I'll hand him his weapon of choice. I can't believe this. I saw how

you manipulated Ethel and Pete, and I still almost fell
into your trap. How could I be so stupid?''

"You're not stupid, dear. Perhaps, like most young
people, you don't give your elders enough credit,'' Cora
said.

Addy looked around the table. "Since I know all about
your diabolical plan, that's the end of it, right?''

The four ladies nodded in unison.

Not for one second did Addy believe them. An eggshell rolled from the table and smashed into smith-
ereens, showering her red sandals with white debris.

The lawyer used by Lorie had forwarded the letter with
a yellow sticky note asking Addy to contact him if she
wanted him to respond to the letter. Addy crushed letter,
envelope and note into a ball which she hurled across
the room. The letter writer had corresponded through
his attorney and signed himself an interested party, but
Addy knew the letter came from her sister's lover. Addy
glared at the crumpled ball of paper under the window.
As if she wanted anything to do with a man who'd
seduced an innocent young woman and abandoned a
child.

Child. That's what he called Emilie in the letter. The
child. Either he couldn't remember Emilie's name, or
he'd never bothered to ask Lorie what she'd named her
baby.

Certainly Addy had nothing to worry about. The letter
merely sought information on Emilie. Addy had no intention of giving him any. He'd never been told Lorie's
sister had custody of Lorie's child. He'd never cared
before. Why should he care now? Let him assume a
couple had adopted Emilie. Couple. Parents. The two
words hammered painfully inside Addy's head. Moving
slowly across the room, she stared at the crunched paper
at her feet, her mind traveling back five years.

She'd arrived home from her first-year job as an elementary school art teacher in Colorado Springs to find a tearful, pregnant Lorie on her doorstep. Four months later, in August, Addy had been in the delivery room when Lorie gave birth. In her cynical moments Addy wondered if Lorie had already made her plans when she named the baby Emilie Adeline.

Two weeks into Addy's second year of teaching, she came home to find the baby with a neighbor and Lorie gone back to California. Finally facing the truth that Lorie wasn't returning, and no longer able to ignore Emilie's piteous wails when left at a day-care center, Addy had resigned her job to care for Emilie. Living frugally, with access to the money Lorie's married lover had given Lorie to buy her silence, Addy figured she could remain home until Emilie started school.

When an unrepentant Lorie eventually phoned, Addy had managed to convince her sister Addy needed more than Lorie's blithe assurance it was OK for Addy to raise Emilie. Addy didn't even like to remember the paperwork, the social worker visits and the courtroom appearances she'd endured before gaining legal custody of Emilie. Legally forever, the lawyer had promised.

Addy brushed aside lace curtains at the window. Record heat, the forecast had said, and nature had delivered. Early afternoon, not so much as a bird moved. No breeze fluttered the aspen leaves or stirred the boughs of the giant blue spruces. Even the wild roses atop the rock wall lining the dirt road looked pale and wilted. The air smelled of dust. Shuttered from the heat, the homes climbing the hillside overlooking the highway up Ute Pass, looked uninhabited. Invaders from outer space might have kidnapped all the residents of Ute Pass. Or perhaps they'd been frightened away by Big Foot, a legendary hairy monster some claimed roamed around Green Mountain Falls.

Big Foot frightened Addy less than the monsters she wrestled on sleepless nights. Such as television images of a small child screaming hysterically as he'd been dragged from the arms of the only mother he'd ever known to be given to his birth parents. Perhaps that mother had believed in legally forever.

A deep male voice sounded from the depths of the big, old house. Sam Dawson. He hadn't found her great-grandmother's clothespin. She'd refused to accept his apologies. She didn't want apologies from him. She wanted his disappearance from the face of her earth. She wanted her talisman back. Fear clogged her throat. She wanted the few, insignificant problems she'd faced a week ago in place of this letter with its daunting possibilities and unspoken menace.

Addy picked the letter up, smoothed the paper, and reread the typed words. The letter said nothing about custody or visitation rights. Nothing in the letter should cause Addy to feel the least bit threatened. She had nothing to worry about. The man might have tons of money and a battery of lawyers, but he didn't care about Emilie. Loving Emilie counted for everything.

Addy walked quietly to the bedroom where Emilie napped. A dirty bandage wrapped the finger where Sweetie Pie, Cora's Siamese cat, had scratched the little girl. Living in apartments, watching every penny, they'd never had a pet. Addy's gaze traveled around the room. No expensive toys littered the floor. No outrageously priced dresses hung in Emilie's closet. Not that judges considered such things. Addy loved Emilie. Lots of children grew up just fine without big homes and pets. Without fathers. Judges knew that.

If Addy were married, Emilie would have a father. Chilled in spite of the warm afternoon, Addy wrapped her arms around her upper body. Judges liked nuclear families. Dad, Mom and the kids. Lorie's lover had a wife. He might have other children.

Addy rubbed her arms and thought about the women's proposal to match her up. Women no longer relied on men to solve their problems. She squeezed her arms, pinching her flesh with her fingers. Emilie didn't need a father.

Emilie mumbled in her sleep. She'd missed a smear of jelly on her cheek when washing her after lunch. Addy loved Emilie so much it sometimes hurt. At first she'd loved her for Lorie; now she loved Emilie because she was Emilie. Addy would fight for the little girl. She wouldn't lose her. She wouldn't let her sister down. No matter what she had to do.

The words echoed thunderously in her head. No matter what she had to do. An image of her great-grandmother's clothespin formed in her mind. Johnson women didn't cry or whine or bemoan the fates. Johnson women did what had to be done. Addy tiptoed from the room. She'd find herself a husband. She'd give Emilie a nuclear family. No judge would take Emilie away from her then.

"Jim Carlson." The voice came from the vine-shaded end of the large covered porch. "Lawyer, thirty-eight years old, used to swing a hell of a baseball bat. Newly divorced, looking for a replacement cook, house cleaner and hostess for his clients. Not to mention he needs a mom for the weekends he has custody of his kids. Teenagers are supposed to be hell to deal with."

Addy watched a hummingbird dart among the tubular blossoms of a patch of scarlet gilia. "I don't suppose there's any hope you'll have the decency to go inside before he arrives."

"None," Sam said. "Jim grew up here, and we go way back. My brothers and I spent most of our vacations and many a school year here in Colorado with

Grandmother and Granddad. You're not in such a hurry to get him alone you can't allow us a little reminiscing, are you?''

In a hurry to go out on her first date in years? With a man she knew only by sight? Equal parts reluctance and trepidation unsettled her stomach. Hours of racking her brain left Addy convinced she needed to marry to secure Emilie's future, yet she couldn't totally repress repugnance at the notion of snaring a husband. Her schizophrenic emotions threw her into the ladies' scheme with less than wholehearted enthusiasm.

Addy was going to dinner with Jim Carlson because she'd drawn his name first. He was Phoebe's candidate. The four women had each written a name on a slip of paper and thrown them in a bowl. Before she'd drawn a name, Addy had made a bargain with the women. She'd give each of the "husband candidates," as Belle called them, two dates. After that, Addy made no promises, her "escape hatch" if the situation proved untenable. Their instant agreement to the stipulation nagged at her like a barely lopsided bead. She knew a flaw existed; she just couldn't find it. The ease with which the women had solved her baby-sitting concerns and the speed at which they'd arranged her first date had not lessened her sense of disquiet. The thought came to her the women shared her worries and concerns about Emilie's future.

Creaking wicker furniture reminded Addy of Sam's presence. "I don't want to discuss my social life with you," she said.

"Why are you going along with this ridiculous idea?"

Addy needed to marry for Emilie's sake. She didn't need to discuss the situation with Samuel Dawson. "What idea?"

"Allowing four old ladies to pick out a husband for you."

"Nobody's picking out a husband for me." Addy would pick. "Apparently everyone up and down Ute Pass thinks I need more of a social life. Cora, Phoebe, Belle and your grandmother persuaded me to allow them to introduce me to some single men they know."

A low hoot of laughter mocked her statement, and the furniture creaked again. "If this is a crack-brained scheme to make me jealous, it won't work, Adeline."

"Carrying around that huge ego must be exhausting work."

Sam moved out of the shadows, and perched on the porch banister near where she stood, his critical gaze sweeping her from head to toe. "I assume wives of small-town lawyers are wearing pink-checked dresses and pearls these days."

Phoebe had selected the outfit. Addy had her doubts. Cora's granddaughter's dress fit so snugly, Addy could barely breathe, much less eat. She had no intention of sharing her misgivings with Sam Dawson. "Don't you have something better to do than harass me?"

"Nope. I sat with Emilie while she ate her supper and now Grandmother and Phoebe are supervising Emilie's bath. Ah, here comes Prince Charming."

Stepping from his car, the balding, slightly stooped man waved. As he climbed the old rock stairs and headed up the sidewalk, Addy noticed the clothes hanging on Jim Carlson's lank body could do with a good pressing. He wasn't handsome, but he had warm brown eyes and looked kind. Addy knew him to nod hello, but they'd never actually met.

The two men greeted each other with the familiarity of old friends. "Of course you know Ms. Johnson," Sam said, "since you're taking her out to dinner."

Addy smiled warmly at Jim Carlson. "Call me Addy."

Sam raised an eyebrow at her, before reminding Jim of a baseball game they'd played years ago. Immediately the two men began rehashing their days of youthful athletics. Addy stood patiently, smiling politely when either man remembered her presence long enough to glance at her.

"Yes, Jimmy's the best player on his baseball team," Jim bragged. They'd moved on to his boys as a topic of conversation.

"You have two boys?" Sam asked. "How old?"

"Jimmy's twelve—"

"Almost a teenager." Sam flashed Addy a significant look.

"Right. And Johnny's ten," Jim said.

"How old is Emilie, Adeline?" Sam asked.

Addy gave him a dark look to remind him she disliked his mocking use of her name. "She's almost five."

Jim Carlson looked at her in surprise. "I didn't realize you'd been married. Isn't divorce difficult?"

"Adeline's never been married," Sam said.

Addy hastily explained Emilie's relationship to her, before gently reminding Jim they had dinner reservations.

"Golly, yes, dinner reservations. Say, I've got a great idea, Sam, why don't you join us? We're going to this Mexican restaurant down the road." Jim lightly jabbed Sam's shoulder. "That's OK with you, isn't it Addy, if Sam joins us?"

"No," she said immediately. "I mean, I wanted to hire a baby-sitter for tonight, because Emilie can be a handful, and Hannah is eighty years old, but she said you'd be home, Sam, if any kind of emergency or anything arose."

"Hannah survived me and my brothers, she'll be fine with Emilie," Sam said. "Besides, Phoebe's here."

"I don't know..." Addy bit her lip. "If one of them fell, and the other had a heart attack or something..."

"Emilie would go to the neighbors. They'll be fine."
Sam moved away from the porch railing.

Addy thought fast, then did a double take, as if just noticing what he wore. "But you're wearing old jeans, Sam. You would feel uncomfortable going with us."

Jim chuckled. "Addy, we're in Colorado."

"Hannah probably has your dinner all prepared."

"She's heating up leftovers," Sam said.

Addy tried again. "I think Emilie plans on Sam reading her a bedtime story." As far as Addy knew, that particular thought hadn't occurred to Emilie, but she'd be ecstatic at the idea.

"Grandmother can read her a story tonight and I'll read Emilie one in the morning," Sam said.

"Emilie has play group in the morning."

"I'll read to the whole play group," Sam said easily. "I'll run in and tell Grandmother I'm going and be right with you. This is a great idea, Jim."

Several hours later Addy stomped up the wooden stairs to the porch and snarled into the dark corner, "Oh, yes, wasn't the three of us having a cozy little dinner a great idea?"

"I excused myself so he could kiss you good-night."

Only an idiot would trust the innocence in Sam Dawson's voice. "I suppose you directed him to park under the streetlight so you could play Peeping Tom." Not waiting for an answer, she went into the dark house and ran lightly up the staircase.

Emilie slept soundly, her stuffed bear hugged tightly to her. Addy kissed the little girl softly so as not to awaken her, then tiptoed from the bedroom, too restless to climb into bed.

The starry night beckoned. Stepping through the long window to the small second-story porch, Addy moved quietly to an ancient glider. No sounds drifted up from below. Sam must have gone inside. The glider protested loudly as she sat down.

The three-quarter moon, climbing into the sky from the east, cast tree-shaped shadows on the road. Crickets sang in the grass. Addy dissolved into the lumpy glider cushions, her muscles relaxing for the first time this evening. Dating had not been part of her life for the past several years, and current rules and rituals bore no resemblance to those of her college years. She'd never dated a divorced man, a fact which undoubtedly contributed to her feeling on edge all evening. Jim Carlson's obvious nervousness hadn't helped.

The only one at the table not nervous had been Sam Dawson. Addy couldn't even begin to guess at his reasons for joining them. Sam might have fooled Jim Carlson into believing he'd accompanied them for old times' sake, but a certain mocking gleam in Sam's eyes when he looked at Addy told her nostalgia had nothing to do with his presence.

A slight wind sighed dejectedly through the evergreens climbing the hillside above the house. Her eyelids sank closed, depression weighing her down. Lorie would have charmed the socks off Jim Carlson and gotten rid of Sam Dawson without mussing a hair on her head. Lorie had come from the womb knowing how to deal with men. What little knowledge of men Addy had learned had disappeared in the last few years. She hadn't minded curtailing her social life for Emilie's sake.

She minded being forced to cold-bloodedly snare an unsuspecting husband. There. She'd finally admitted to the feelings roiling nastily in the pit of her stomach. Her youthful dreams of marriage had centered on love, not security.

Addy mentally shook herself. She was twenty-eight years old. The time had come to face reality. Prince Charming wouldn't ride up to sweep her and Emilie away

on his shining white charger. For centuries women had
been marrying men for all kinds of reasons other than
love. Plenty of successful marriages were based on security. It would be enough for Addy.

And for her husband? She ruthlessly shoved aside any
qualms of conscience. She wasn't asking for charity. Even
if she couldn't love the man she married, she'd be a good
wife to him. She knew she wasn't beautiful, but men
didn't look at her and turn to stone, either. Her husband
would have a reasonably good cook and, despite Sam
Dawson's opinion to the contrary, an able housekeeper.
Addy pleated skirt material between her fingers. He'd
have a willing woman in his bed at night. In return for
security, she'd give him companionship, loyalty and
commitment.

Loud scuffling noises came from below the porch.
Addy's thoughts flew to the bear that had been sighted
recently in the neighborhood, but before she could panic,
a dark head popped up above the second-story porch
floor.

"It's like riding a bicycle," Sam said with satisfaction. "One never forgets." He pulled himself higher,
and swung both legs over the railing. "Harry and I used
to climb up here to get away from Mike when he was a
little guy. He was the world's worst pest. Hard to believe
he's a medical doctor now."

Addy wanted to shove him off the second-story porch.
"Did you have to scare me half to death?"

"Scare you? Did you think Jim had come back to
attack you?"

"Of course not." In spite of herself she added, "You
shouldn't lean against the railing."

"OK." Pushing her to one side, he joined her on the
glider, propelling it back and forth with his long legs.
"Nice evening."

Addy chose to misinterpret his meaning. "No, it wasn't. When you and Jim Carlson weren't discussing past history, each trying to top the other's stupid stories of adolescent behavior, and discussing people I've never heard of, you encouraged him to tell us all the sordid details of his divorce." Sam took up far more than his share of the glider. Through her full skirt, Addy felt his warm thigh move against her leg as he pushed the glider.

"You can never have too much information, Adeline. If you're planning to marry the man..."

"Ms. Johnson to you," she said automatically, "and I never said I planned to marry him." A cool breeze sprang up, riffling her skirt and sending chills down her arms. She shivered.

Sam draped an arm around her shoulders. "I suppose you had visions of you and Jim, a cozy little twosome over Margaritas, and sitting in the moonlight with ol' Jim's arm around you."

"We met this evening for the first time." Addy doubted ol' Jim's arm would have the effect on her ol' Sam's arm did. Only because Jim Carlson had never kissed her. Sam Dawson was a jerk. A jerk whose lips touching hers gave pleasure. She instantly denied the thought.

Sam tightened his arm; his hand firmly held her shoulders, preventing Addy from rising. "I'll bet Jim would have kissed you. He would have raised your face like this, and..." Sam lowered his head.

She didn't mean to go willingly into his arms. Nor did she intend to part her lips at the slightest urging of his tongue. The glider jangled as Sam shifted, and Addy found herself locked in two strong arms. She was in no danger of falling. There was no reason to wrap her arms around Sam's neck. His solid chest warmed her breasts, excited them, made them ache for something more. Sam's fingers, firm and warm, held her face still as he explored the moist reaches of her mouth. He tasted of coffee and after-dinner peppermints. He smelled clean. And masculine. There was nothing soft or weak about the well-rounded bottom lip pressing against Addy's mouth.

He abandoned her mouth to sear a trail of kisses down her neck and press a light kiss against the pulse rapidly beating at the base of her throat. He nibbled sensuously along the ridge line of her shoulder. Addy's every breath brought her sensitized shoulder skin in contact with the thin gingham fabric of her dress, damp from his mouth. The unexpectedly erotic sensation jolted her body. Sam scattered kisses on skin bared by her open collar, and slid the top two buttons free. Her breasts grew heavy, and a fluttering need unfurled deep within Addy.

Sam slid a long finger down the partially unbuttoned front of the dress, the end of his finger almost reaching the tip of her breast. Addy breathed shallowly, her whole body poised for the moment Sam would ease the ache swelling up in her breast. He slowly moved his hand deeper into her dress. Could he feel her pounding heart? Blindly she sought his lips with her mouth.

"The problem is..." Sam's mouth moved against her lips. "Jim's hung up on his wife." He lifted his head. "Do you want to be a substitute for Lois?"

Addy went utterly still. Sam's hand rested inside the top of her dress, his thumb curled around the hardened tip of her breast. Her legs lay across Sam's hard thighs, and his arm held her close against his chest. The light from the street lamp failed to illuminate this high, and the pale oval of his face hovered indecipherable above her. She prayed the dark as successfully concealed her face.

Deliberately she removed his hand, catching her breath as he brushed his fingers across her tight nipple in passing. She didn't make the mistake of thinking he'd touched her unintentionally. "What makes you think I couldn't make him forget Lois?" Her steady voice did her proud. Swinging her legs off his, she shook off his arm and stood up. "If I wanted to."

"You heard the way he went on and on about how wonderful Lois is and how the divorce was all his fault and how he misses his boys. Just because he practically drooled every time he looked at you in that skintight dress with Grandmother's pearls hanging between your breasts doesn't mean he wants to marry you."

Addy gripped the metal frame behind the glider cushions, her hand wrapped tightly around the metal slat, her fingernails digging into her palm. "Nobody said I wanted to marry him."

"Oh, I believe that."

An indecipherable note in Sam Dawson's voice put Addy on alert. She remained silent.

"The 'a' key jumps on my grandmother's typewriter," Sam said casually. "The letter I received was written on her typewriter."

Addy understood immediately. The discovery had absolutely convinced Sam Dawson that his mother and grandmother, with Addy's connivance, had written the letter decoying him out to Colorado as a potential husband for Addy. Furious, but apparently reluctant to take his anger out on his mother or grandmother, he'd targeted Addy.

Sam Dawson hadn't kissed her because he found her irresistible, or sexy or even mildly appealing. He'd kissed her to satisfy some twisted notion of revenge, although Addy couldn't even begin to guess how one connected to the other. Unless he planned to seduce Addy before convincing his grandmother to throw her out into the street. Did he think Hannah would call Addy immoral and drive her away because of a few foolish kisses?

Down the street a dog barked sharply. A passing breeze carried the pungent odor of a marauding skunk. The strident screech of the glider as Sam shifted his weight wakened Addy from her trance-like state. She crossed the narrow porch floor to the low window telling herself no matter how despicably Sam Dawson behaved, he had no power to disrupt her life. The hoot of an owl mocked her simple-mindedness. Addy stepped through the window, slammed it shut and secured the lock. Sam Dawson had climbed up to the second-story porch. He could darned well climb down.

"More pancakes," Emilie chirped.

"No fair. You and your aunt cheat." Sam jabbed his fork into a stack of pancakes. "How can I eat more pancakes than you if she's making your pancakes smaller than she's making mine?"

"You have Sam pancakes. I have Emilie pancakes," Emilie explained seriously.

Sam watched Emilie as she liberally poured syrup on her pancakes. "What time's our play group?"

"Our play group?" Addy asked coldly.

"I told you I'd read to the kids this morning."

Addy eyed him narrowly. Not one bit did she trust Sam Dawson's friendly, pleasant behavior. Hannah's presence wasn't forcing him to be civil, because his grandmother wasn't at the breakfast table, preferring to eat cold cereal earlier.

Flipping a pancake, Addy wished she'd had time to shower before breakfast, but she'd been running late. The fact she'd suffered a sleepless night had nothing to do with Sam Dawson. She flipped another pancake. And again caught a whiff of the masculine scent clinging to her skin.

If only he'd go back to Boston. Emilie liked him too much. Like a new toy, Addy assured herself. Once he

left, out of sight, out of mind. Addy looked at her niece.
"If you're finished, run upstairs and wash up and brush
your teeth. I'll be up as soon as I finish breakfast and
the dishes, OK?"

"OK." Emilie scrambled out of her chair and ran to
Sam's side. "One, two, three, four, five, six, eight," she
chanted. "I ate eight. Did I beat you?"

"Seven, eight," Addy said.

Emilie shook her head. "No, ate eight."

"Give me your hands," Sam said. "Let's name these
fingers who need their faces washed." He held a little
finger. "We'll call this guy One, this guy Two. He's
Three..."

Emilie caught on quickly. "Four, Five, Six, Eight."

Sam frowned down at the last-named finger. "This
finger is crying. He's very sad."

Emilie's eyes grew big. "Fingers don't cry."

Sam held her finger up to his ear and pretended to
listen. "He's crying because his name is Seven. He says
the next finger is named Eight. Let's name them all
again." When Emilie had done so successfully, Sam said,
"You have to promise you won't forget Seven again. I
can't stand to hear Seven's crying."

Emilie solemnly promised.

"OK, run up and wash eight fingers and two thumbs.
No, don't even think about kissing me with that syrupy
mug. You've got more syrup outside your mouth than
I put inside mine."

Emilie giggled and ran from the room.

Addy served up the last of the pancakes and sat to
eat. She refused to like this man.

"I want to apologize for last night." Sam rested his
elbows on the table, cradling his coffee mug in his hands.

"Kissing a woman out of revenge going too far even
for you?"

"I meant intruding on your date. Kissing you had nothing to do with revenge." He acted surprised she would think so. "I'm a healthy, normal male. You're a healthy, normal female. The moon was bright. Naturally we wanted to kiss each other."

Addy set the syrup down with a thump. "I didn't want to kiss you. I wanted to know what you were up to."

"A probing investigation," he said dryly.

Addy couldn't help blushing, which further infuriated her. Kissing her stupid was bad enough; taunting her the next morning about her enthusiastic cooperation was despicable. Doggedly she forced unappetizing pancakes down her throat.

Sam broke the prolonged silence. "You and Emilie have been good for Grandmother," he said unexpectedly. "She has a new bounce to her step. As reluctant as I am to admit it, I hired the wrong kinds of women to be Grandmother's companions. They made her feel older. You and Emilie make her feel younger. I appreciate that, and to show my appreciation, and prove I have no hard feelings about the letter, I'm going to help you."

"Help me what?" Before Sam could answer, Addy realized what he meant and glared at him. "Forget it. Emilie and I aren't charity cases. We manage just fine. We get room and board here plus I teach crafts classes several times a week at the community center, and I make a little extra on the jewelry I sell. We don't need or want any money from you or anyone else." Even to Addy, her words sounded harsh and ungrateful. Belatedly she added, "Thanks anyway."

Sam put down his coffee cup and quietly applauded. "Great speech. Now you've gotten it out of your system, let's discuss my offer. I'm not offering you money. I'm offering you practical help. Grandmother said the ladies agree you need to get married, so you're looking for a husband for you and a father for Emilie."

Addy slapped her fork on the table. "Emilie doesn't need a father." Before he could dispute that, she added a defiant lie. "And I'm not looking for a husband."

"Sure you are." He tapped his chest. "And I'm your man."

CHAPTER FOUR

EVERY jaw muscle Addy owned slackened completely. She tried three times before finally managing to speak. "You can't be serious. Marry you?" The look of shock on Sam's face brought Addy to her senses. "Your sophomoric humor must make you a hit at office parties." She grabbed the plate in front of him, ignoring he was still eating, scraped the pancakes and bacon into the sink and flipped a switch. The loud grinding noise of the garbage disposal covered up the garbled sounds Sam made. She was sick and tired of his harassment. If she'd felt light-headed after his announcement, it was only because his stupid announcement had stunned her. No woman in her right mind would want to marry a conceited, egotistical, contemptible, mean-spirited, twisted, revengeful creep.

A hand reached around her and switched off the disposal and the water. A stark silence filled the kitchen. "I probably could have approached the subject a little better," Sam said.

"I doubt it." Addy managed to refrain from slamming the plates into the dishwasher. "I'm sure you got exactly the reaction you wanted." Squeezing the kitchen sponge with a vicious twist, she hurled it in the direction of the sink.

"I can explain. I—"

"Forget it." Addy stormed from the kitchen.

Hannah came out of the front parlor. "What's going on? I heard you shouting over my news program."

63

"Nothing." Addy dashed up the stairs. Sam stayed to spin lies for his grandmother. Addy had no intention of telling Hannah she'd actually believed, for a second—a very tiny second, Addy reminded herself—Samuel Dawson had proposed marriage. As if she wanted to marry anyone with such a cruel sense of humor. Addy certainly did not want to marry Sam Dawson.

Maybe, for a fleeting instant, she'd pictured life married to Sam. Safe. Emilie with two adults responsible for her. No more financial hardship. No worries about a judge taking Emilie away from Addy. No sacrificing herself on the altar of matrimony to provide security for Emilie. Not that marrying Sam wouldn't be a sacrifice. Certainly his kisses had nothing to do with her momentary lapse of sanity. If he never crossed her path again, Addy'd be ecstatic.

She was not ecstatic when she saw him leaning on the newel post at the bottom of the staircase when she and Emilie descended the stairs. Sam watched them, a wary look on his face.

"Now what?" Addy snapped. "An irresistible urge to engage in more cute tricks from your repertoire?"

"Play group."

"If you think I'm going to let you contaminate a group of innocent little children, think again."

"Addy." Emilie tugged on her aunt's hand. "Addy maddy?"

"Yes." Addy stomped toward the front door.

Emilie tugged on Addy's hand again. "I don't like you mad."

Hearing the wobble in Emilie's voice, Addy halted and looked down. "Sweetheart, I'm not mad at you. I have a headache." That part of her reassurance to Emilie was true. Addy knew her head would explode into a million pieces any second now.

"In that case," Sam said, holding open the front door, "you'll definitely need my aid and assistance this morning."

About to deny she'd ever need anything from Sam Dawson, Addy swallowed her words at the glowing expression on Emilie's face.

Sam knew better than to gloat. He helped Emilie with her seat belt in the backseat of Addy's ancient automobile and sat sideways in the front seat listening to the little girl's chatter. Leaving Addy to drive and to consider the chances of turning left in front of an oncoming car without hurting anyone except the passenger beside her in the front seat.

A witless ground squirrel dashed across the road daring Addy to squash him into the dirt. She swerved to avoid the small animal, but if the squirrel had been Sam Dawson... Two black and white magpies flew by, loudly squawking, their long tails streaming behind. Beside the road, fuchsia-crowned thistles grew next to taller cow parsnip. Cow parsnip with its umbrella-shaped clusters of white flowers belonged to the parsley family, as did the extremely poisonous water hemlock. Addy entertained thoughts of fixing Sam Dawson a hemlock salad for dinner.

The Joseph and Anna O'Brien Community Center, a solid, old two-story yellow brick building located in the middle of the small town sprawled along Fountain Creek, had housed O'Brien's Drugstore in earlier days. Hannah's parents, Joseph and Anna O'Brien had started the drugstore in 1924, later hiring Peter Harris as a pharmacist. Hannah claimed she'd taken one look at Peter and fallen instantly in love. They'd married and taken over the drugstore when Joseph died, but it'd stayed O'Brien's Drugstore. Hannah's and Peter's only daughter, Sam's mother, chose to be an actress, so when Peter died, Hannah donated the building to the town along with start-up funds for the community center. Small family drugstores had gone the way of the dodo bird in this age of discount stores and chains, Hannah said. Addy often wondered what it was like to have one's family history interwoven with a town's history.

Released from her seat belt, Emilie dashed toward the building. Sam stood on the sidewalk looking up, his hands stuck in his pockets. "I worked here. Swept floors, stocked shelves, made deliveries on my bicycle, waited on customers. Harry and Mike worked here, too. We saw the miracles of medicine. And the failures," he added almost to himself.

Addy detoured around him. She already knew from Hannah those failures had sent Sam and his brothers to college determined to find ways to fight disease. Sam's two brothers had turned to medicine, while Sam immersed himself in the biochemistry field where he dealt with arcane matters beyond Addy's expertise. Even if Sam Dawson were the world's greatest philanthropist, he wasn't likable.

A rufous hummingbird whistled past, his throat reflecting iridescent orange in the sunlight.

"Sam!" Emilie stood impatiently at the door. "Hurry up!"

If Emilie had had buttons on her pink playsuit, she would have burst them as she proudly showed off Sam to the other children in the play group. Hollywood would never know what it'd missed, Addy thought cynically, watching him act out the various characters in the story he read aloud. The circle of children hung on his every word. Hopefully they remembered to breathe.

"What a hunk," whispered a mother standing beside Addy. "Who is he, where did he come from, and why, oh, why, am I a happily married woman with two kids?"

Addy briefly explained Sam's relationship to Hannah Harris.

"He's so good with the kids. I see Emilie has adopted him. He's not wearing a wedding ring." The woman glanced down at Addy's ringless fourth finger. "Are you and he . . . ?"

"Certainly not!" Addy said explosively.

"What a shame." The woman moved off.

It wasn't a shame. It was a blessing. Even if Emilie might not agree. Emilie would be crazy about anyone whose eyes crinkled every blasted time he smiled at her. He wore another blue shirt. Pure vanity. He must know blue shirts made his eyes look bluer. He probably bought them by the truckload. Sitting on the floor made it easier for a certain blond little girl to hang around his neck. Sam Dawson needed female attention so desperately, he'd flatter a four-year-old to get it.

One of the mothers took over the play group, leading the children in a song and some playful exercises. Sam staggered over. "Water," he choked, his hands grabbing his throat.

Addy filled a paper cup with water at the sink and thrust it at him. His shirt, unbuttoned at the top, exposed lightly tanned skin, and as he tipped back his head and drank, the working of his throat muscles fascinated Addy.

"Thanks." Sam tossed the crumpled cup into a nearby trash container. "Now, about this morning." He pitched his voice low, for her ears only.

"I don't want to talk about it."

"I didn't mean to—"

"Get my girlish hopes up? You didn't." A bottleful of aspirin wouldn't dent her headache. Addy smiled as Emilie looked in their direction. Emilie waved at Sam and giggled.

"I meant," Sam said in a low, measured voice, "I'm the man to help you find a husband."

"What!" Several mothers swung around to look at them. Addy smiled weakly before turning her back on Sam. "I'm not looking for a husband, and if I was, I wouldn't need your help," she rasped over her shoulder, moving away.

Sam trailed behind her. "I thought we agreed you need a husband and Emilie needs a father."

"We agree on nothing. Leave me alone and mind your own business." Grinding her molars as two mothers grinned meaningfully at her, Addy fled into an adjacent storeroom.

Sam carefully shut the door to the empty room as he followed her in. "Try viewing your situation calmly and objectively."

"The only thing I want to view is your back leaving."

"I'm not going anywhere until you listen." Grabbing her shoulders, he maneuvered her against a set of floor-to-ceiling shelves. "I know you want to get married. I can help you."

The letter the lawyer had forwarded flashed across Addy's mind. As much as she disliked Sam, listening to him couldn't hurt, and Emilie's future took precedence over Addy's pride and personal prejudices. Locking her hands behind her to hide their shaking, Addy said, "OK, talk, but make it quick."

"Have you heard of synergy? It comes from a Greek word and stands for what happens when two distinct forces work together. You and I working together can create synergy."

"I don't need you or your synergy."

"Call it a strategic alliance. Forget the mawkish sentimentality associated with romance and look at all facets of your situation. Simply put, I'm in the business of anticipating and solving problems. I know about developing business deals, generating information and how to use it, and I'm experienced in filling key positions.

Factor that in with me being a man—" he looked guile-lessly at her "—and what do you have?"

"A total idiot, who's made the mistake of thinking I'm as big an imbecile as he is. This has nothing to do with finding me a husband. You're planning a petty campaign of harassment in retaliation for that letter you received. I've got news for you, Dr. Samuel Dawson, Ph.D., you can't reduce me to your infantile level, so quit obsessing over revenge and run back to Boston to show poor, ineffective scientists how to save us from bugs and germs taking over the world."

"You're safe. No bug or germ would be foolhardy enough to take you on," he said dryly. "I had to make all kinds of arrangements to break free, and the office knows how to reach me, so I'm staying with Grandmother for three weeks."

"Stay three years for all I care, but stay away from me and Emilie."

"You can't forget about that kiss, can you?"

"What kiss?"

He ignored a question they both knew was rhetorical. "Grandmother and her friends rounded up some can-didates for your husband, but they failed to put any mechanism into place to sort through the candidates and decide which best suits your needs."

"Maybe they had the crazy idea I might want to choose my own husband. If I was thinking about getting married."

Sam shook his head. "You're too emotional. Once I decide on our man, that's where my other area of ex-pertise comes into play. I'm a man, so I know what other men want. I know how to identify selling points, how to position sellers in the market, and I know about packaging. I'll structure the deal to meet our winning candidate's particular wants and needs."

"Packaging? Structure the deal?" Addy asked tightly.

"Make marriage to you irresistible to him. Negotiate. Find out what he wants. Men have different likes and dislikes when it comes to women. Is he a ponytail and jeans kind of guy or does he prefer sleek up-on-your-head hairdos and slinky evening gowns? Is he looking for a mother for his kids, or a woman to entertain his clients, or someone hot to share his bed? The ladies applauded the brilliance of my idea." He didn't bother with false modesty. "I'm now an official member of the team."

Speechless, Addy squeezed her eyes shut and contemplated hysterics. Screaming at the top of her lungs and drumming her heels against the metal storage shelves held enormous appeal.

"Head still pretty bad?"

She sucked in a little air and opened her eyes. The eyes hovering so close to her exhibited sincere and deep sympathy. Another award-winning acting performance. "Let me make something plain to you." She spit out the chilly words. "In exchange for living in your grandmother's house, I cook for her, shop for her, run errands for her, and generally help with tasks she finds difficult. My duties do not include entertaining her grandson." Pushing him aside, Addy marched over to the door and opened it. "Furthermore, when and if I decide to get married, my husband will be selected by me, not by committee to fill a key—" She snarled the last word "—position, and I won't be packaging myself by dressing up like Little Bo Peep or Lady Godiva!"

Sam looked beyond her. "Lines from my mother's latest play."

Addy whirled. The play group session had finished, and a large number of fascinated mothers and children populated the recreation room. Addy's angry words reverberated from the walls.

Sam chortled as he climbed into the car. "If you could have seen your face."

Addy jammed her key into the ignition.

"Sam, how come Addy yelled at you?" Emilie asked from the backseat. "Was you bad?"

"No, I wasn't bad. I was brilliant. Don't stare at me when you're driving, Adeline. Watch the road."

Addy jerked the car back into the proper lane.

"Addy don't like people calling her Adeline."

"Is that true, Adeline?" He laughed. "Guess you're right, Emilie. She doesn't even hear me when I call her Adeline."

"I'm Adeline, too. Emilie Adeline."

"You look like an Emilie Adeline," Sam said.

"Addy says I look like Momma. Momma is in Heaven with angels," Emilie said matter-of-factly.

After a long minute, Sam cleared his throat. "I'm starving. What's for lunch?"

"My arrangements with Hannah do not include fixing your lunch," Addy said coldly.

He fixed his own lunch. And lunch for everyone else. Tuna salad sandwiches on whole wheat bread with orange slices and carrot sticks on the side. When Emilie took one bite of her sandwich and turned up her nose, Sam turned lunch into a lesson on fueling the human body machine, ghoulishly and graphically describing the heart squirting blood into little tunnels called arteries. Riveted, Emilie absentmindedly ate every bite.

"Sorry about the mustard. Hope it washes out of Emilie's clothes." Sam wiped mustard from the table, chair and floor. "Emilie's hand-eye coordination isn't up to squirting mustard into straws. Is this mess why you sulked at lunch?"

"I did not sulk. I had no interest in joining a conversation about stomachs beating up food."

"Still have a headache? Emilie and Grandmother went down for naps." He handed her a dirty glass. "Why don't you?"

"Why don't you," Addy responded, spacing her words distinctly, "get out of my life? I don't want your advice. I don't want your help. I don't want to know about little blood cells running through my body doing cleaning chores or fighting battles. I don't want to know about selling points or packaging. I don't want any kind of alliance with you, strategic or otherwise. What I want is for you to go away and leave us alone."

A kindly fate granted Addy her wish for almost two hours. Knowing Sam's absence was too good to last, Addy wasn't surprised when he walked into the kitchen later that afternoon.

He sniffed the air. "What smells like melting plastic?"

"It's tough to poison someone with a sensitive nose like yours. I should have fixed almond pudding with ascorbic acid."

"Ascorbic acid is vitamin C. I think you mean cyanide, a poison associated with a bitter almond scent. I hope that smell doesn't have anything to do with dinner."

"If you object to my cooking or a little smell in the kitchen, go away." The oven timer dinged, and grabbing pot holders, Addy removed a shallow cardboard box from the oven. Wires draped over the box's rim held patterned beads of various sizes, shapes and colors. Carefully avoiding touching the hot beads, she set the box and its contents on a rack.

Sam scrutinized the beads. "Wild colors."

Addy switched off the stove, picked up the box of beads and headed up to her rooms. "My customers like wild colors," she said with an edge to her voice.

"My customers like honest, objective, worthwhile advice." Following her to her sitting room, he set his black leather briefcase on the floor and cleared space on the table for a small gray case which opened to reveal a laptop computer. "Let's get down to business." He sat on a fancifully painted chair.

"We have no business." Finding a husband wasn't business. It was the rest of her life. "Just because Hannah and the others sanctioned your idiotic scheme, you needn't think I'll allow you to treat me like some kind of germ you're experimenting with."

Sam leaned back. "Join the modern world, Adeline."

"Scientists always think progress is better than history. They aren't always right."

"Don't sneer at science." He pointed to the beads cooling on the table. "Where would you be if PVC hadn't been developed and artists hadn't pushed the envelope on its applications?" Without waiting for an answer, he deftly moved his fingers over the keyboard. "I've already entered some information. Belle's candidate is next. John Christain, assistant manager of Woodpine Lodge, the hotel Belle sold to the big chain. Age, thirty. A quick-rising wonderboy, highly thought of by the chain's home office." He pulled manila folders from the briefcase on the floor and piled them beside his computer. Extracting one file, he handed it to Addy. "Here's a snapshot. Belle say he's a dreamboat, but we don't care about good looks."

Addy set the folder down unopened. Even for Emilie, she didn't know if she could carry out this crazy scheme. Marriage to her had always meant love and commitment.

A long white envelope on the table caught her eye. Another letter. Phrases seemed to leap from within the closed envelope. They were imprinted on her brain. "Like to meet with the child's adoptive parents...discuss some issues...interest in the child's welfare..." The innocuous letter shrieked of potential disaster.

Addy took a deep breath and repeated what was quickly becoming her mantra. Partners in arranged marriages could find happiness. When she found the right man, she'd do her best to make the marriage a successful one.

First she had to get rid of Sam Dawson. Addy Johnson was not a blip on his computer screen. "You haven't collected all your data. If I was looking for a husband, you'd have to consider my needs and wants, too."

Sam nodded, his hands poised about the computer. "That's reasonable. Go ahead, name them."

Addy leaned her elbows on the table, propped her chin on her hands, and stared at the opposite wall, her mind inventing. "He'd have to like purple. And be rich. I'm tired of shopping at thrift stores." She ignored the narrow-eyed look Sam gave her. "Drive a red sport car, and have a large house, so I can keep all my things for Emilie for when she grows up."

Absently Addy reached for a pair of thin rubber gloves and pulled them on. "Be dependable. I want to know he'll always be there for Emilie and me. He won't take off and never return."

She kneaded a hunk of black polymer clay. "Have a huge family. The kind you see on television with sisters and cousins and aunts and uncles who like each other and have big, fun, family reunions. They'll love and cherish Emilie and never make her feel like an outsider. She won't wear hand-me-down clothes unless she wants to, and everyone will care if she receives straight A's, and want to see her star in high school plays and rejoice when she wins an art contest..." Her voice trailed off. "You're not putting this down."

Sam studied her across the table. "Grandmother said your parents were killed in a car accident when you were a kid."

"Not really a kid. I was thirteen." She pointed to the keyboard. "He'll have to promise no interference with how I raise Emilie. And he'll have to understand Emilie will always come first with me. I may have let..." Addy swallowed. "I won't ever let Emilie down. He'd have to accept that."

"Whom did you let down?"

"No one. Next, he'd—"

"Grandmother told me your sister committed suicide. You don't blame yourself for that, do you?"

"She was an adult. If she chose to decide she had no one worth living for, that could hardly be my fault." Addy pounded her fist on a mound of clay. "Lorie was eleven when we lost our parents, and I watched out for her and stood up for her until the day I left for college. It was only two years. I didn't abandon her." Addy ripped the ball of clay into small hunks. "I expected her to join me after she graduated from high school. It wasn't my idea she run away to Hollywood." Hearing her voice rising, Addy took a deep breath. "I don't know why we're talking about that. You hate living in the past." She smiled brightly. "That should be enough data to keep you busy. Just look for a man who likes purple and is rich."

After a moment Sam asked, "Do you want children?"

"Emilie would love having brothers and sisters." Removing her rubber gloves, Addy added black eyebrows to a clay face.

"Good sex," he said in a measured voice as he typed. "Or would you prefer great sex with passion?"

Addy felt red color sting her cheeks. "Highly overrated."

"Speaking from experience?"

"Lorie claimed great sex as the rationale for losing her head over a married man, having and abandoning his baby, and running back to sleep with him. Delete passion. I don't want kisses that force a person to engage in amoral behavior."

Sam closed his computer with a snap. "I don't think I would have liked your sister."

"Lorie was beautiful, bright, talented, funny, and clever." Addy studied her black fingers. "Her smile acted as a magnet on every male in the vicinity." Addy's voice softened. "I'm angry with her behavior, but I loved her very much. For years it was the two of us against the world, and then she was gone." Addy swallowed hard over the painful lump in her throat. "I don't suppose I'll ever get over missing her."

Sam pushed back his chair and came around the table. "I'll bet you tried to give your sister everything you thought she needed. The same way you try to give Emilie what she needs." He removed the clay from Addy's hands, setting it on the table. "I think it's time someone gave you what you need."

Addy thought about resisting as his hands on her shoulders pulled her to her feet. "I don't need anything."

"Yes, you do, Adeline. You need kissing."

That was the dumbest thing she'd ever heard, Addy thought, clutching at Sam's upper arms with hands which tingled from kneading clay. She didn't need kissing. She needed to be held and comforted. She needed... Humiliation surged hotly through her veins. She flung her hands from his shoulders. "I told you before. I don't want or need your charity."

Blue eyes hardened. "What you need is to knock that self-pitying chip off your shoulder."

"You're the one who asked me about my sister." Sam Dawson tricked her into saying things she'd never said to another living soul, and then accused her of self-pity. "If missing someone who's died is feeling sorry for myself, then I feel sorry for myself. Obviously if everyone you know dropped dead tomorrow, it would have no impact on your life whatsoever."

"I'm not talking about a little healthy grief. Everyone needs to grieve. Even an irritating, stubbornly independent aunt who's constantly ranting and raving that she needs nothing." Reaching for Addy's single braid, he wrapped it around his fist, tilting her head back until she met his eyes. "Afraid it's a sign of weakness if you admit to needing anything?"

"Charity comes at too high a price." Addy squarely met his gaze. "I can't afford to gamble that I might like it, might become dependent on it. What happens when charity stops? Emilie didn't have the best start in life. To survive, she'll have to be strong. I'm the only one she has to teach her strength."

Sam shook his head. "You've given Emilie the best kind of start in life. You love her." He slid his hands around Addy's neck, his thumbs resting in front of her ears. "You're strong enough that graciously accepting a little charity isn't going to weaken you. Not that it matters in this particular instance, because a kiss is not an act of charity, Adeline Johnson."

"What is it?"

"I've always found one scientific demonstration is worth pages of text." He lowered his head.

Addy's mouth opened under his gentle, determined urging. Fingers splayed on her head curved gently against her scalp as Sam pulled her close. For a moment Addy forgot to breathe, then, remembering, she inhaled an intoxicating masculine scent overlaid with the flowery plastic odor of her clay.

One kiss wasn't enough. Her fingers dug into his arms. She needed more of his firm lips slanting, opening over hers. Hesitantly she curled her tongue around his, and shook with the heat her action unleashed deep within her. Pressing closer to his solid body, she felt his pounding heart. Or her heart.

Sam's firm, unyielding thighs, hips, chest imprinted themselves on her body. As the soft one, the yielding one, she melted into him, losing all sense of where she ended and he began. He was home and family, security, safety.

Except he wasn't. He was the man who wanted her to marry someone else. Addy pulled away from his kiss, pressing her forehead against his shoulder. She had to say something light and amusing. Anything to let him know his kiss meant nothing to her. No easy words came to her rescue.

Sam stirred. "Maybe I was wrong. Maybe a kiss is an act of charity." His arms tightened as Addy stiffened. "No, don't go critical on me. I meant you're a very giving, generous person." His hands rested lightly on Addy's shoulders as he gazed contemplatively down at her. "Under other circumstances I'd be interested in exploring the depths of your generosity, Adeline Johnson, but you're living in my grandmother's home, raising a child, and looking for a husband." A tinge of regret flashed across his face before he smiled crookedly. "Great sex with passion isn't highly overrated, and I'm certain a woman who paints her walls purple would refuse to settle for anything less, but I'm afraid your husband is the one who'll have to convince you of that. You're a woman who needs commitment, not a two-week stand." He brushed a stray hair from her face. "I hope you appreciate how much I'm going to hate myself tonight for being honorable."

Addy pushed away from his loose embrace. "I'm supposed to thank you for being honorable when you spout the most disgustingly arrogant and patronizing drivel I've ever heard? Did it ever occur to your little pea-size brain I don't have the slightest interest in playing bedroom games with you? I let you kiss me because you're like water torture. Constant, unremitting drip, drip, drip. If you want to call letting you have your own way so I could get rid of you, generosity, go ahead." She moved to sit on the sofa before her shaky muscles failed her. "But remember, I'm the one who wanted you to run back to Boston, and I'm the one who wanted you to mind your own business. And before you bring it up, if I was ever so stupid as to think marrying an arrogant, conceited egotist like you was a good idea, which I wasn't, I'd have long ago changed my mind. If I were getting married, I'd marry anyone but you."

"Good." Sam swept the folders from the table into his briefcase and retrieved his computer from the table. "While I might be tempted to sleep with you, I have every intention of marrying you off to some poor slob who doesn't place a high priority on honesty in his wife."

"Are you calling me dishonest?"

"Lying is dishonest. You enjoyed that kiss, and you didn't kiss me to get rid of me."

"You're the one who claimed I needed you to point out what men want. Maybe now you'll admit I already know, and you'll leave me alone."

"Adeline, the only thing your kiss told me is you have less experience than the average teenage boy."

The tinge of pity in his voice infuriated Addy. "That's not true. All right," she added quickly at the look on his face, "I admit I'm out of practice. It's been a few years since I bedded the football team, two fraternities and the marching band." Her raised chin challenged him to call her a liar.

His mouth barely curved at the corners. "Belle said to tell you John Christain will pick you up tomorrow night to escort you to an outdoor jazz concert. I assume an accomplished woman of the world such as yourself will know enough to wear something other than the tight, wildly provocative dress you wore when you went out with Carlson. A sweater and slacks would do. If you have to wear pearls, try little earrings, instead of that pearl rope of Grandmother's calling attention to your breasts."

"I don't think," Addy said in a dulcet voice, "a man who runs around in a blue shirt covered with black fingerprints is qualified to critique my wardrobe. I suggest you change it before Hannah sees it, or she won't be quite as impressed with how honorable her grandson is as you are."

"At least," Sam said, a muscle jumping in his tight-clenched jaw, "my shirt is buttoned." The door closed behind him.

Addy looked down. She'd replaced the cheap buttons on the fuchsia blouse with polymer buttons. She'd made them too small. Her blouse gaped open, exposing a wide expanse of freckled skin.

She hated Sam Dawson. Didn't she? Dejection settled over her as she faced an unpleasant truth. She should hate him, but she didn't. Emilie had tumbled head over heels in love with Sam, and Addy was in danger of becoming infatuated with him herself. Infatuation. A disease for fools. Why couldn't science come up with a cure for that?

Addy stared at the wood-paneled door to the hall, her stained fingers moving restlessly at her side. A deep azure blue paint covered this side of the door. The same blue as Sam's eyes before he kissed her. She didn't like him. His looks simply appealed to the artist in her.

His sensual mouth with its full bottom lip was all wrong for his face. Addy raised a trembling hand to her mouth. She wished she had bedded half the male population at the university when she'd been there. Maybe then she wouldn't find Sam Dawson's kisses so devastating.

Addy's panicked gaze flew around the room before settling on a framed picture of her sister. Her sister's confident smile calmed Addy down. And reminded Addy of the one thing which mattered. "Don't worry, Lorie. I'll take care of Emilie for you. I won't do anything foolish."

*　　*　　*

John Christain was tall, with fashionably cut black hair and gleaming white teeth surrounded by dark stubble. He drove a burnt yellow sports car, and his dark brown eyes gleamed with appreciation as he swiftly looked Addy over. Appreciation and a quickly disguised sense of relief.

Addy smiled at him as he set up a lawn chair beside hers near the edge of Antlers Park in Colorado Springs. Discordant notes came from the improvised stage as the musicians warmed up. John Christain had undoubtedly dreaded the evening. He wasn't the only one experiencing relief. There were no worries about an undesirable third on this date. Emilie had personally appointed Sam her baby-sitter for the evening.

Pleasant, charming, and amusing, John entertained Addy with witty stories of hotel guests and diverting tales of his travels around the world. He thought Colorado the back of beyond, but submitted his current job was the price one paid for advancement. An advancement, he took pains to make clear, which was practically guaranteed.

Glancing over Addy's shoulder, John's face grew puzzled.

"What's the matter?" she asked instinctively.

"That man and his little girl. They're acting like they know me, and I swear, I've never seen them before in my life."

Slowly Addy turned her head, knowing full well what and whom she'd see.

Ten feet away, Emilie jumped up and down, waving with both arms. "Surprise!" she hollered. "Surprise!" Dissolving into giggles, the little girl collapsed on a blanket spread over the grass. Her baby-sitter smiled indulgently.

Addy turned back to a mystified John Christain and mustered a weak smile. "My sister's little girl. I'm raising her."

His gaze traveled from Addy to Emilie and back to Addy. "That her father?"

"Her baby-sitter." The look of disbelief on John's face told Addy her brief explanation had created more questions than it answered. Perversely, she chose not to enlighten him. She was tired of baring her life for one and all to dissect.

Excited giggles warned Addy she and John had a visitor. Two soft arms stole around her neck. "Sam and me gonna hear music." Before Addy could respond, Emilie was gone.

Not for long, of course. During the concert, Emilie practically wore a path in the grass between Sam and Addy. If Sam exerted the slightest effort to control his charge, it was not evident. John managed to maintain his composure in the face of stiff provocation. No doubt he had a great deal of experience in dealing with difficult hotel guests. And their equally difficult children.

Not to mention totally useless baby-sitters.

CHAPTER FIVE

STANDING on the porch steps, Addy turned and held out her hand to John Christain. "Thank you for a lovely evening. I enjoyed the concert, and dinner afterward was delicious."

He captured her hand and pulled her closer. "I thought I was doing Mrs. Rater a favor, but she did me the favor. I'll pick you up tomorrow night about seven."

Addy stifled a sigh. John Christain presumed a great deal, but one couldn't blame him. Belle had practically served Addy to him on a silver platter. "That would be nice," she said politely, compelled to agree by her promise to go out twice with each man who asked her. "What did you have in mind?"

"You." He gave her a slow, sensual smile which reeked of practice. His brown eyes reflected the gleam of the porch light.

Addy's heart beat at its usual steady rate. Nothing throbbed, nothing pulsed. "Me?"

"I don't like going blind into any situation," he said. "I asked around. Everybody in town knows you're a single mother with no man in the picture. It must be harder'n Hell to find anyone around here who shares your mature, healthy attitude toward taking care of your sexual needs." John lightly traced the lines in her palm.

Addy's normal breathing never altered. "Emilie is my niece," she said coolly.

"You can call her your uncle if you want. Believe it or not, I grew up in a small town. I know the lengths a person has to go to to appease narrow-minded hicks.

83

That's why I'm ideal for you." His smile deepened. "Meaningless sex suits me perfectly. I'll meet your needs, keep your secrets, and then be on my way with no awkward emotional entanglements."

"I think you'd better be on your way now." The hard voice came from the other side of the screen door.

John Christain's gaze flicked past Addy. "The baby-sitter, I presume." His gaze returned to Addy. "Sorry, Addy, I guess I didn't see the whole picture." Before Addy could set him straight, he turned and walked to his car.

"We can cross him from our list," Sam said.

"Thank you for nothing." Opening the screen door, Addy barreled past Sam. "John is now convinced you and I sleep together. It will be all over town we share more than your grandmother's house." She stomped up the stairs, spitting words over her shoulder. "I could have handled him. Didn't harassing me at the concert provide you with enough amusement?"

"I thought you'd approve of a little practical experiment." Sam's voice masterfully conveyed hurt feelings and misunderstood intentions. His dejected footsteps trailed Addy up the stairs.

Addy reminded herself his parents made their living on the stage. "What was your experiment supposed to prove? That an adult male can act like an overgrown, spoiled child?"

Pushing open the door she tried to shut in his face, Sam followed her into her sitting room and flopped down on her sofa, his legs hanging over one end. "That's the problem with an experiment where all the variables can't be controlled," he said, rearranging the pillows to stack them under his head. "Bound to have unexpected side effects. Such as Christain turning out to be a sex-crazed adolescent disguised as an adult."

Addy shut the bedroom door after checking on Emilie. "I'm talking about you. You deliberately set out to ruin my evening."

Sam gave her an astonished look. "You're angry with me?"

"I allowed Emilie to call you her baby-sitter tonight because Hannah and Belle would be here if you had any problems. You did not have my permission to take Emilie anywhere."

"I didn't realize I needed a written note from 'Mama' before I exposed Emilie to a little culture."

"Culture," Addy snorted. "You took Emilie to the concert to make mischief and have a good laugh at my expense." She curled her legs beneath her in an armchair. "You knew how she'd act."

"Like a four-year-old. Face facts, Adeline. When you climbed into his expensive sport car, Christain wiped off your fingerprints. A man like that doesn't want any snotnosed kids. Everything about him from the body sculpted in the hotel's fitness center to the tanning-saloon tan says he's fixated with himself. I'll bet he spends a fortune getting his hair cut and the clothes he wore came straight from a catalog on what the best-dressed man wears for leisure. Christain isn't the type to buy a station wagon and shoot hoops with his kids."

"You don't know—"

"I didn't. I do now. That's why I ran my little experiment with Emilie. To test my hypothesis that Christain dislikes kids. Which he does. He hides it well, but even you couldn't have missed how he flinched whenever Emilie came near him."

"Considering you brought peanut butter and jelly sandwiches and no damp cloth to clean her hands after she ate, anyone with the barest minimum of good sense would have fended her off."

"Something I'm curious about—"

"You're worse than Emilie. Curiosity is a disease with you. Remember, curiosity killed the cat."

"Curiosity also led to penicillin, landing on the moon, and—" he slanted an ironic glance at the brown and red smears on his blue chambray shirt "—peanut butter."

"Not to mention the atom bomb," Addy said. "If you scientists wouldn't be so insufferably curious, and occasionally thought about where your snooping was taking you, the world wouldn't be cursed with car radios blaring at every stoplight and plastic bottles littering the landscape."

Sam grinned. "Good try, but you're not diverting me down that path. Scientists are also persistent and single-minded, so you may as well satisfy my curiosity. There's something strange about these poor slobs' willingness to be sucked into this scheme. Christain's proposition indicates Grandmother et al aren't hawking you as a prospective wife, so what's the hook? Why do these guys eagerly get in line? No offense, Adeline," he added, in a patently superficial concession to her feelings.

"What's wrong with lonely men wanting to meet single women?" Addy hadn't asked what pressures the four women brought to bear on the men. She hated to see grown women lie. "Just because you took one look and decided bubonic plague was more attractive than me, you needn't think all men find me repulsive."

"Annoyed because I avoided Mother's and Grandmother's trap, or mad because I refuse to sleep with you?"

"If I wanted to sleep with anyone," Addy noted with pleasure, "lovers are a dime a dozen, as John proved tonight."

Sam frowned at her. "You brought his behavior on yourself, wearing that black outfit. You might as well have doused yourself with male-attracting pheromones."

"You told me to wear trousers."

"I didn't tell you to wear skintight pants."

"They're stretch pants," Addy said stiffly. Belle had borrowed the outfit from a teenage neighbor. "They're supposed to fit snugly. It's not my fault men drool like Pavlov's monkeys every time they see a female between the ages of six and sixty."

"Snug." Sam made a disgusted sound. "A flea couldn't fit in there with you. And your sweater is three sizes too small."

"I didn't realize you'd earned your doctorate in female fashion. What did you expect me to wear—a lab coat?"

"At least," he said coldly, "a lab coat wouldn't outline and accentuate every freckle on your body."

Sick and tired of his constant taunting about her freckles, Addy jumped up from her chair. "Go away." She locked her hands behind her to keep from slugging him. "It's late and I'm tired."

Sam rose slowly from the couch and moved to stand in front of Addy. She'd left her hair hanging loose about her shoulders tonight, and he reached for a long strand, wrapping it around a finger. "You should have taken some science classes in school."

Addy stood very still. Except for her heart, which tripled its beat. Not because of fear. Because—she didn't know why. She forced herself to say, "I took biology and chemistry and—"

Sam took possession of her lips. When he eventually lifted his head, he said, "You must have flunked them."

Addy's mouth tingled from his kiss. The artist in her wondered if it was possible to duplicate the fascinating shade of blue of his eyes. On the heels of that crazy thought came the realization his kiss had scrambled her brains. She took a deep breath, concentrated on a button in the middle of his blue shirt, and somehow picked his last comment out of the air. The direction of his thoughts drove the wobbles from her knees. "If you're intimating there's some kind of chemistry between us, you're wrong." Taking hold of his wrist, she freed her hair. "I only let you kiss me because I didn't want you to cause a scene and awaken Emilie."

"Chemistry," Sam repeated thoughtfully. "Labeling what's between us a chemical reaction probably isn't too inaccurate. I'm willing to admit you hold a weird fascination for me."

"Although I'm intensely gratified to hear I'm on a par with dead frogs and earthworms, I'm not interested in being stuck under your microscope, so go practice chemistry with one of your Boston beauties. And I got A's in all my science courses."

Laughter crinkled the corners of Sam's eyes. "Believe me, you're much more kissable than frogs and worms." Proving it, he dropped a light kiss on her nose. "Even if you don't know Pavlov used dogs to study conditioned response. He trained them to expect food every time he rang a bell, and eventually they salivated whenever they heard a bell even if no food appeared."

"I knew that." She practically shouted the words at the closing door.

"Addy, where's Sam?" Emilie stood in the bedroom doorway, rubbing her eyes, Sam the Bear hanging by one paw.

"He's gone to bed. Where you should be."

Emilie trailed Addy back into the bedroom and hopped obediently into bed. "I like Sam. Do you?"

"Yes," Addy lied. Sam Dawson was the most insufferable, irritating person she'd ever met. Thinking about him and his kiss, her mouth softened and weird feelings ran riot deep in her stomach. Remember Pavlov and his stupid slobbering dogs. Sam's kisses were merely bells making her drool. Which meant she had no more brains than Belle's fat, slobbering, black lab, Lovie.

*   *   *

A perfunctory knock at the open door announced Sam's arrival. "Adeline, I want to talk to you right... What are you doing? It stinks of paint in here."

Emilie rushed to greet him, recklessly waving her paintbrush. "We's painting." She dragged Sam into the bedroom.

Addy rolled paint on the bedroom wall. She had nothing to say to Sam Dawson, at least nothing she could say in front of Emilie. Furthermore, she had no desire to listen to anything he had to say. He appeared to be struck dumb.

"Isn't it be-yoot-i-ful?" Emilie gave a heartfelt sigh.

"It's rather..." Sam hesitated. "Pink."

"Fairy Princess Pink," Emilie announced with deep satisfaction. "The paint man made it jus' for me."

"No," Sam shook his head, "the paint man told you the wrong name. It's definitely not Fairy Princess Pink."

"Is so," Emilie insisted.

"No, it's Emilie Pink."

"Emilie Pink!" The little girl took a couple of joyful hops, then wailed in dismay. "Addy! I boo-booed." She pointed to a fat smear on the wall made by her waving brush.

Addy studied the splotch. "Try painting a heart over it."

"OK." With great concentration, Emilie turned the smear into a huge heart-shaped blob. Finishing, she put her brush in the paint and wiped her hands on the old shirt she wore backward over her clothes. "All done," she announced. "Now you."

Addy laid the roller in the paint tray and walked over to Emilie's side. With long flowing strokes she brush-painted a few words on the wall. A small heart formed the bottom of her exclamation point.

Emilie bounced and clapped her hands in approval.

Sam, watching curiously, read the wall. "'Emilie loves Addy. Addy loves Emilie.' You're not going to paint this wall?"

Emilie looked at him with horror. "Addy has to. It's a secret message. Peoples can paint and paint but the message will...what will it, Addy?"

"Endure for all time."

"That," Emilie said triumphantly. "Then it's a happy room and Addy won't cry at night."

"Does Addy cry at night?" Sam asked.

"Emilie Adeline," Addy said at the same time. "We've discussed this before. You are not to tell people family stuff."

"He's Sam, not peoples."

"Out of the mouth of babes," Addy said dryly, before addressing Emilie. "Go wash the paint off you. You have a pink nose and a pink chin."

"Grandmother said to tell you she's sewing on some buttons if you want to help," Sam added.

"Buttons!" Emilie tore from the room, her aunt's shout to wash following her.

"She doesn't actually help. She loves to play with Hannah's beautiful buttons," Addy said into the enormous silence filling the room. She carefully spread more paint on the wall before nervously blurting, "Everybody gets colds and the sniffles once in awhile. That's all it was." More wide swathes of pink paint covered the old white paint. "If you supposedly-brilliant drug people would invent a cure for the common cold, the rest of us wouldn't sniffle at night." The excessive flow of words wouldn't stop. "Even you must sniffle when you have a cold."

"Were you crying because of something I said last night?"

"I haven't given a second thought to anything you've said to me since we met." The task of loading the roller with paint required minute attention. "I wasn't crying. Emilie heard me when I had a cold. And not last night."

"Money troubles? Paint, even Emilie Pink, is expensive."

"Hannah bought the paint in exchange for me re-papering her bedroom. I don't have money troubles. People buy more than they need to be happy anyway." Putting down the roller, Addy started to pick up the ladder.

Sam put his foot on the bottom rung of the ladder, firmly anchoring it. "Did the letter you received make you cry?"

Addy froze. "What letter?"

"The one I evidently grabbed off the table with my folders the other night. I found it in my briefcase a few minutes ago and read it before I realized it wasn't mine."

"The address on the envelope didn't give you some kind of clue?" Then she remembered sticking the envelope in her drawer. It hadn't occurred to her to check if the letter was inside. She grabbed the ladder. "Move your foot."

Sam leaned his elbow on a ladder rung. "I assume the anonymous correspondent is Emilie's father."

"Emilie has no father." She kicked the ankle on the ladder.

"Ouch!" He grabbed his ankle, and Addy swiftly moved the ladder as he hopped around the room. "The guy has finally wakened to his responsibility. You ought to be cheering."

"We've managed fine without him." She brushed a strip of paint along the top of the wall. Her unsteady hand left a pink streak on the ceiling. Addy tramped down the ladder for a wet rag to repair the damage.

Sam's eyes narrowed to dark slits. "What are you afraid of?" he finally asked. "Having to share Emilie?"

"The only thing I'm afraid of is I'll never finish painting these walls. Too many interruptions." Her furious scrubbing turned the small pink smear into a large unsightly blotch.

"You're making it worse," Sam said.

"Your incredible powers of observation must be why you had to get out of scientific research." Addy stomped down the ladder again, filled her brush with paint and stomped back up the ladder. Hearts exploded from her paintbrush to march defiantly across the corner of the ceiling.

"Father or not, there's no way the man can take your place with Emilie," Sam said.

"Tell that to the courts just before they rip her away from me and give her to him because he happens to have some of the same genes." Retrieving the roller, Addy blindly swabbed the wall. "She's a person with feelings, not a thing."

"I thought you had custody," Sam said slowly. "Didn't you tell me you have a paper the man signed giving up any rights he might have as Emilie's father?"

"You think that matters? He's worse than slime, but he slept with my sister, so some people think that makes him Emilie's father no matter how many stupid papers he signed."

"It sounds to me as if you're getting hysterical over imaginary bogeymen. Try thinking rationally with a little less emotion and a little more reason."

"I do not need a lecture on logic." Addy slammed the ladder against the next wall.

Sam moved out of her way. "Name one thing you know about Emilie's father which would make it remotely possible he'd want custody of Emilie."

"Who knows why slimebags do anything?"

"In other words, you have absolutely no shred of evidence he's changed his mind and now wants Emilie. You don't even know if whoever wrote the letter is Emilie's father."

"Who else could it be?"

"Your sister lived in Hollywood for a couple of years. She undoubtedly had other friends. Some of them must have known about the baby and wondered what became of it."

"They might have wondered, and might even have tried to find out something through the lawyers, but they wouldn't have issued sinister threats saying I needed to discuss issues concerning Emilie or tried to entice me to meet them with vague promises of me benefiting by such a meeting. Why not identify themselves?"

"Oversight. He or she dashed off a quick letter—"

"Two," Addy said flatly.

"You received a second letter?"

"You read the second letter."

"Get me the other one."

Tempted to challenge Sam's right to curtly order her around, Addy reminded herself Emilie's welfare came before all else. She walked to the dresser, pulled out the letter and handed it to him. She waited impatiently as he scanned the letter, then slowly reread it, a frown on his face. "Well?" she challenged.

"What did your lawyer say?"

"I don't have a lawyer. Lorie hired this man to handle the custody details, but he was never my lawyer."

"I think you ought to take the letters to Jim Carlson and get his advice. He may be small-town, but he's a good lawyer."

"I don't need a lawyer." Addy's fingers tightly clenched the paint roller. What was she supposed to pay Jim with? A necklace? She swallowed the bitter laughter in her throat.

"I know lawyers are expensive." Sam echoed her thoughts. "I would be—"

"No! I do not want money from you." Jerking the letter from him, she thrust it back in the drawer.

"It wouldn't be charity. More of a loan."

"I don't need your money. I have everything under control." Addy slapped paint on the last wall. Sam watched her, but she sensed his thoughts were elsewhere. She wished he'd lurk elsewhere. Painting walls wasn't a spectator sport. He stood in front of the window, and his elongated shadow crawled up the ladder with her. A passing breeze brought in the smell of sweet clover to compete with the strong paint odor. Any whiff of masculine scent had to be a figment of her imagination.

Without warning Sam said, "Oh, hell," in an exasperated voice. "That's what this ridiculous husband-hunting business is about, isn't it? You really are looking for a husband."

"I've never said so. You're the one babbling about selling points and position in the marketplace."

"For Pete's sake, Adeline, I was joking."

"Joking." She looked down from the top of the ladder.

"Not exactly joking," Sam qualified. "Teaching a lesson."

"A lesson." She had to quit repeating everything he said. As if repeating the words clarified anything.

"My mother and my grandmother married young and had children at a young age," Sam said. "They are convinced everyone else should do the same. While I understand that Hannah at eighty wants to see her great-grandchildren, it's hardly a compelling reason for me to get married. They disagree. For the past five years, since I turned thirty, they've been relentless in their drive to marry me off." His entire body radiated irritation as he paced the small bedroom.

"I've told them I'll get married when I'm good and ready and I neither want nor need their assistance in the matter," he said, "but they are determined to play matchmaker. You wouldn't believe how many women they've introduced me to, or the convoluted schemes they've tangled me in. They've involved Dad, my brothers, my friends, even co-opted my employees. I blew my top after the last little episode, and they promised they'd quit. Dragging me out here on a false alarm demonstrated I put too much faith in their promises. I decided to teach them a lesson."

Addy opened her mouth as Sam braced a shoulder against the wall by the ladder, then snapped it shut and doggedly slapped paint on the upper portion of the wall.

"I considered romancing you, then jilting you at the last minute, after they had the wedding planned. I figured you deserved it for aiding and abetting their scheming."

Addy resisted throwing the paint roller at him. "Since you didn't follow through with the plan, I assume you have a better side."

He gave her a wry smile. "What I have is a healthy respect for the kind of scene my mother would throw if I pulled such a trick. Not to mention a deep fear, if I went that far, that somehow I'd find myself married to you."

Addy pressed the paint roller against the wall so hard her wrist ached. "I can see where the thought might give you pause."

"Try nightmares." He'd missed her sarcasm. "After considering the matter at great length, I devised the perfect plan to circumvent their scheming and frustrate the hell out of them. The only way they could accuse me of deliberately sabotaging their scheme would be to admit they'd been scheming again, in spite of their promises."

The blood drained from Addy's head, and she grabbed the top of the ladder for support as the extent of Sam Dawson's treachery became clear. "You decided the best

way to ruin their plans was to pretend to work enthusiastically to marry me off to someone else.'' Her voice
sounded unnaturally high-pitched. ''No wonder you
thought your plan perfect. Your counterfeit cooperation
allowed you to sabotage my dates.'' How dare he
undercut her efforts to safeguard Emilie's future for his
own selfish, petty reasons? Forcing her hands to release
their death grip on the ladder, Addy carefully climbed
down to the floor.

''Adeline, it doesn't take a nuclear scientist to figure
out not one of the men on the ladies' list is serious
husband material for you. I assumed,'' he added, ''your
dating was part of some grand plan to make me wild
with jealousy.''

He condemned himself with his own words. With grim
determination, Addy reloaded her roller with paint. He
may have destroyed Emilie's future, but he wouldn't destroy her pleasure in her room. No matter how transi-
tory that pleasure proved to be.

''I suppose the letters frightened you and you thought
having a husband would make a difference if it came to
a custody fight over Emilie,'' Sam said.

''It's none of your business.'' Addy fiercely attacked
the remaining section of white wall with the roller. She
wanted to fling the paint can at his head.

''I did some research. Phoebe hinted to Jim Carlson
that taking you to dinner would make Lois jealous. The
management of the hotel where Christain works owes
Belle a few favors for smoothing their way to getting
permission from the town council for the addition. They
repaid her with Christain.''

''Jim used me to get back his wife and John used me
to further his career?'' Addy asked in a tight voice. ''The
others?''

Sam shifted his weight to his other shoulder.
''Grandmother chose Tom Erickson, the football coach

over at the high school. Five minutes of research told me he's practically engaged to the German teacher at the high school. He wants the job as coordinator of summer activities at the center next summer." Sam paused. "Grandmother is involved in the hiring process."

Addy took a deep breath. "And Cora?"

"She contributed Perry Wilson. I couldn't find her hold over him, but he's an overaged flower child who's been married who-knows-how-many-times and currently dabbles in some kind of hocus-pocus New Age medicine. Hardly marriage material."

Had her desperate search been a game to everyone but her? Addy sopped up more paint and carried the roller to where Sam stood.

He raised an eyebrow at the roller. "The ladies selected frivolous candidates. I assumed you knew that. The only logical conclusion a reasonable man could come to was that the stated purpose—to match you up with one of those men—was not the real purpose. What are you planning to do with that paint?"

"Paint the wall behind you." She gave him a stony look. "Again."

"Sorry. I thought it was dry." Sam dabbed futilely at the pink on his shirt. "It's as clear as the paint on your face, Adeline. Grandmother and the others never intended any of those men to fall for you. They were either red herrings to avert any suspicion on my part or intended to make me jealous. Grandmother wanted me to fall for you. Which explains her enthusiastically welcoming me to the matchmaking team. She figured my involvement would mean spending more time with you. It obviously never occurred to her I might resist your multiple charms."

Addy's tightly-wound restraint snapped. With a quick sweep of the roller, she painted Sam from head to toe in Emilie Pink.

After a stunned silence, Sam loosed a string of potent swear words. Appalled by her loss of control, Addy stood frozen. Searching her stunned brain for something to say, she failed to turn up a single word.

Sam confiscated the roller. "Get me a rag."

The snarled demand rekindled her fury. "Get your own rag."

"Fine." He yanked at the front of the man's shirt she wore. The ancient, threadbare, oft-laundered garment surrendered without a fight. Fabric parted and buttons flew. Wadding up the ragged front section of Addy's shirt he'd ripped loose, Sam wiped his face.

At the dangerous look in blue eyes under paint-smeared brows, Addy turned to run. A locked fist around her braid stopped her in mid-flight. "Let go of me," she hollered.

"Having two brothers taught me—" Sam reeled her back "—turnabout's fair play."

"Don't talk to me about fair play." Addy struggled to break free of Sam's ruthless grip, at the same time attempting to cover her old bra and bare skin with the ragged edges of her shirt. "Not when you've been making a game of my life."

"Why didn't you tell me the truth in the beginning?" he asked defensively, momentarily loosening his hold.

Addy only needed a moment. Wrenching free, she rushed for the bedroom door. Sam seized a fleeing shirttail, and Addy half turned to slap away his hand. Her feet tangled with the slick protective plastic drop cloth on the floor and slid from under her. Stepping backward to recover her balance, Addy stuck her foot in the nearly empty gallon paint can, her arms windmilling wildly. One elbow tangled painfully with the aluminum ladder. The other rammed Sam in the midsection as he lunged to catch her. The ladder, Addy and Sam all hit the floor at the same time. It was Sam's bad luck to be on the bottom. It was Addy's bad luck to fall sandwiched between the ladder and Sam's outstretched body.

"You OK?" Sam shoved the ladder off Addy.

"Yes." Addy stiffened as he ran his hand over her body. "I said I'm OK." Kicking away the paint can, she tried to scramble to her feet.

Sam snaked an arm around her, flipping her so she lay flat on her back beneath him. "You're not going anywhere until we talk." He caught her hands in one of his.

In spite of the clownlike pink splotches decorating Sam's face, Addy didn't have the slightest urge to laugh. Breathing heavily from her abortive efforts to escape, she struggled to free her hands. "You don't want to talk. You want revenge."

"You think I want revenge because you slapped paint on me?" Bracing his upper body with his elbows, his lower body held her against the floor, his legs easily corraling hers.

"You're not seeking revenge because of a couple of drops of paint. You blame me for forcing you to come to Colorado, so you've tried to make my life miserable from the minute you walked into this house." Gathering her muscles, Addy heaved in an effort to dislodge him from her body.

Sam's weight barely shifted. "I want to know if you were part of the plan to trick me into marrying you."

If he moved his shoulder a couple of inches lower, she could sink her teeth deep into his muscles. What was a little paint on her molars compared to the satisfaction of venting her fury? "How many times do I have to tell you I'm not the least bit interested in you and I had nothing to do with that letter you received?"

He raised a pink-frosted eyebrow. "Next you'll tell me you're not even looking for a husband." Before Addy could speak, he said roughly, "Don't bother. You think if it came to a fight with Emilie's father over custody your position would be stronger if you were married to a responsible citizen. I'm considered a responsible citizen, single and, according to my female relatives, should be looking for a wife. It doesn't take a Ph.D. to figure out the three of you conspired to lure me out here so you could somehow convince me to marry you."

"I'd never marry a man as stupid as you. Your ego is so huge there's no room in your head for a brain." Catching her second wind, she tried again to eject him. "Move. My body's going numb."

"Lucky you." His lips twisted. "The way you're wiggling, numbness is the least of my problems." He ran a finger along the inside of her elbow.

Addy barely controlled a shiver down her spine. The paint on Sam's jeans seeped through her shorts and dripped on her bare legs making her legs, sticky and damp. His paint-soaked shirt brushed against her skin. Missing the front of her shirt, she should be cold. She wasn't. The late afternoon sun heated the room. The smell of latex paint swirled about her. The thudding of his heart echoed in her ears. Not his heart. Her heart.

"Hell," Sam said, rubbing a thumb over one of her high, prominent cheekbones. "I'm going to have to kiss you."

She raised no objection. Not because she wanted to kiss him. Because he wouldn't have listened anyway. She closed her eyes. Enhancing her other senses. The paint odor receded, replaced by Sam's now familiar scent. Firm lips, warm lips, opened over hers. He released her hands and she wrapped her arms around him, cradling his head with one hand. His short hair tickled her sensitive palm. With her other hand she stroked his back, absorbing into her being the warmth and security of taut, muscled strength.

Sam removed his mouth from hers. "You've got pink freckles." He brushed a fingertip over her closed eyelids, then slowly traced a path from the corner of her eye down her cheek.

Addy opened her eyes. Sam's face hovered inches above her, his left eyelid drooping sensuously. He should have looked ridiculous with paint outlining his sunken cheekbones and squared-off jaw. He looked delicious. "So do you," she said. "Have pink freckles."

"Freckles, hell." White teeth gleamed in a garden of pink. "Adeline, every square centimeter of my epidermis is pink."

"Not just any pink. Emilie Pink."

"Who wouldn't want to be painted Emilie Pink?"

"My point exactly."

"I'm glad to hear you say so." Sexy, teasing laughter lit up his eyes.

Blue eyes could be so compelling. Dangerously so. Distracted by her confused reaction, Addy didn't immediately grasp the significance of Sam's remark. The sound of a can being rolled across the floor brought her to her senses. "No!"

"But it's Emilie Pink." Amusement tinged his voice. Recapturing her hands, he imprisoned them in one of his above her head. With his other hand he dragged the paint can nearer.

Her frontless shirt gaped completely open. "You'll be sorry!" Addy gasped as Sam smeared a handful of cold paint on her upper chest.

"No, I won't." Sam laughed softly. "This is fun."

Addy sucked in half the air in the room as he spread the paint, warming it with his outspread palm. She didn't stand a chance fighting against the hard body pinning her to the floor. Maybe refusing to struggle further would ruin Sam's fun, and he'd quit torturing her. Turning her head away, she closed her eyes.

Shutting out Sam's laughing face failed to make him go away. The heavy masculine thighs laying on hers heated her lower regions. Her breathing grew rapid and shallow as Sam rubbed on paint in ever-larger circles, his hand moving slower and slower. Friction between his palm and her skin warmed her blood, sending it pulsing through her body. "Squirting," Addy muttered, in a desperate attempt to replace one image with another. "Like mustard."

Sam gave a low laugh. "Pouring." Sensual awareness edged the softly spoken word.

A cold rivulet of paint ran between Addy's breasts. Tickling her. A sensation of a different sort replaced the tickling sensation as Sam trailed the tiny river of paint with his finger.

"I never finger-painted as a kid." He pushed aside Addy's bra and circled her breast with his finger. "I didn't know what I was missing."

Electricity sizzled through her body. Addy's eyelids shot open. Sam wore a look of total absorption as, with slow deliberation, he painted the tip of her breast. Addy's stomach rioted. She forgot how to breathe.

"That looks like fun. Can I play?" Emilie's chirping voice came from the bedroom door.

"I think only two can play the game Sam and Addy are playing." Hannah's voice couldn't have been dryer.

Sam released Addy's hands and rolled off her, but horror kept her pinned to the floor.

"Your sense of timing is impeccable, as always, Grandmother. Or did Adeline send an invisible signal summoning you?"

The chill in his voice raised goose bumps on Addy's bare flesh. His outrageous implication ignited her temper and destroyed her good sense. Covering herself as best she could with the remnants of her shirt, Addy sat up and tossed porcelain smiles around the room. "Sam's right. Your timing is wonderful, Hannah. You can be the first to congratulate us. Sam just asked me to marry him, and I said yes. Emilie, say hello to your new daddy."

CHAPTER SIX

"DADDY?" Emilie asked in an uncertain voice. "What do you mean, Addy? Is Sam my daddy?"

"He wouldn't really be your daddy." Addy avoided looking at Hannah. "Do you remember me explaining, since your mama is in heaven, I'm your substitute mama?" When Emilie nodded, Addy went on. "Since we don't know your daddy, the man I marry will be your substitute daddy, the same way I'm your substitute mama."

Emilie smiled shyly at Sam. "You gonna be my substitute daddy, Sam?"

"Ask your aunt. She's the one with the convenient answers."

The curt words wiped the smile from Emilie's face. "Sam's yelling at me."

"That's the first thing you have to learn about men, Emilie," Hannah said briskly. "They tend to yell when they're not sure what's going on."

"I know exactly what's going on," Sam snarled.

"See what I mean?" Hannah took Emilie's hand and turned her away from the door. "Let's go fix ourselves a root beer float and plan the wedding. Sam and Addy need to clean up."

Their voices had barely disappeared down the staircase before Sam turned on Addy. "Very clever, Ms. Johnson. Do not make the mistake, however, of thinking I'll marry you."

He'd made the mistake. From the moment of his arrival Sam Dawson had gone out of his way to disrupt and ruin her life. Not once had he considered anyone's concerns but his own. He didn't care if Addy lost custody of Emilie. All he cared about was his own selfish, bachelor status. A status he was about to lose. Through his own self-centered actions.

Addy aimed a dreamy, vacant smile in the vicinity of his right ear. "Emilie will make an adorable flower girl in a dress of Emilie Pink polished cotton. I can whip up one on the sewing machine. I'll wear my grandmother's wedding dress. What kind of flowers do you think I should carry?"

"Did you hear me? I am not marrying you." Frustration ran grittily through his voice.

"Of course you are," Addy said reasonably. "How could you possibly refuse after you ripped off my clothes and assaulted me on my bedroom floor? I'm thoroughly compromised since you were seen painting my half-nude body by your eighty-year-old grandmother whose total sexual activity before her marriage probably consisted of a few chaste kisses, and by my four-year-old niece who will certainly entertain her contemporaries at play group with all the fun details."

"Don't exaggerate," he retorted. "Men don't marry women because they were seen kissing them. I'd like to remind you who started this fiasco by smearing me with paint."

"I dabbed a little bit of paint on you. I didn't force you to rip off my clothes. I didn't make you kiss me."

"I admit I find you intriguing and sexually attractive." With an expression of distaste he picked up the discarded piece of Addy's shirt and wiped paint from his fingers. "But building a successful marriage takes more than a mutual urge to copulate."

Addy's face flamed. "I don't have any such urge."

"You fake it well." Ignoring her indignant sputtering, he added, "Adeline, you can announce all you want that I asked you to marry me. But I didn't. And I won't."

"You don't have to announce it." Deliberately misunderstanding him, Addy bared her teeth in a parody of a smile. "I think it's safe to say our engagement has already been announced. I'll bet Hannah is on the phone to your mother right now. If you didn't bring a suit, you'll have to buy one. Naturally I'll want to get married before you return to Boston."

"I am returning to Boston." Sam spit the words from between clenched teeth. "Alone. In a little over a week. You have until then to straighten out this mess."

"I don't think it's such a mess."

"You will," he said grimly, "by the time I get through with you. One week," he repeated, "to make crystal clear to my grandmother I did not and will not ask you to marry me." Sam strode from the room, rage pouring from every inch of his body.

Addy hoped he saw himself quivering like a deer in the spotlight with a target painted on his backside. When he calmed down enough to use those brilliant brain cells he was supposed to be overendowed with, he'd see he brought the whole mess on himself. Him and his selfish, egotistical plan to teach his mother and grandmother a lesson.

He'd sealed his fate when he'd accused Addy of conspiring with his grandmother so Hannah would catch them in the act of whatever. For a man with a Ph.D., Sam Dawson possessed the brain of an amoeba. Any idiot could have seen the unexpected appearance of Hannah and Emilie at the bedroom door had totally stunned and embarrassed Addy.

Any idiot but one who possessed an ego the size of Pikes Peak. The nerve of him believing she'd set him up to catch him in a compromising position. He was the

one always preaching they lived in the modern world.
Women didn't play those kinds of games, if they ever
had, which she doubted. She'd set out to find a husband,
but she'd always intended to be honest with her potential bridegroom. Who wanted to marry a man she
had to trick into marriage? Not Adeline Johnson.

At least, she hadn't. She might not feel so vengeful if
he'd demonstrated the slightest bit of contrition over
sabotaging her dates and harming her plans. Which he
hadn't. She wasn't about to risk losing Emilie because
Samuel Dawson played juvenile games. The man was
supposed to be a grown-up. He should be able to deal
with his mother and his grandmother on an adult level.

The sun slid behind the towering hillside, and shadows
crept in to cover the floor and steal warmth from the
air. Addy's muscles refused to move. She dreaded facing
Hannah. Sam's face must have informed his grandmother Addy's announcement of their upcoming nup-
tials came as a complete surprise to him. Addy pushed
aside speculation on Hannah's thoughts when the older
woman had walked into the bedroom, and reminded
herself humiliation paled beside the worries about Emilie.

Worries intensified by Sam's actions. Shunting aside
her fears, Addy focused on her anger. Anger gave her
strength to go toe to toe with Sam Dawson. Making the
decision to marry for Emilie's sake had been difficult
enough. Forcing herself to actively seek out single men
for the purpose of matrimony had taken every ounce of
courage she possessed. All for naught. Thanks to one
selfish, overbearing, so-called genius.

Sam Dawson ranted and raved about logic and reason.
Logic and reason said Sam Dawson owed Addy a
husband. She'd darned well tell his grandmother he did.
After she cleaned up the painting mess and showered.

*   *   *

"Congratulations, dear. I know you and Sam will be as happy as Frank and I were."

Stunned, Addy looked up to see an ebullient Cora enter the crafts room. Belle and Phoebe followed her, adding their best wishes. Addy pinned an accusatory gaze on the woman bringing up the rear. "Hannah, I thought we agreed not to tell anyone."

"I changed my mind." Hannah shut the door to the crafts room. "You can't expect them to waste their time trying to match you up with someone if you're planning to marry Sam."

"I certainly wouldn't want anyone to waste time like I've been wasting it going out on these so-called dates you arranged."

"I'm sorry they haven't worked out," Phoebe said.

"I'm sure they worked out just fine. Was Lois Carlson jealous enough to run back to Jim as you planned? I understand John Christain thought dating me would advance his career. Did you really think the much-married hippie, Perry Wilson and I would make the perfect couple? Did Tom Erickson plan to bring his almost fiancée along when he took me out?"

"What kind of allegations are you making?" Phoebe asked slowly. "Admittedly I debated if it was too early for Jim to start dating, but I finally selected him because he's proven himself a good father. Yes, Perry Wilson, has been married twice, but he's hardly a hippie. He sells natural foods and vitamins and told Cora he wants to start a family."

"I know Tom Erickson loves kids and if he's dating anyone special I hadn't heard about her," Hannah said. "As for John Christain, the rest of us objected, but Belle insisted since we'd made our choices with Emilie in mind, she thought someone ought to consider your needs. She thought you'd find him fun."

"I said you'd find him sexy," Belle said.

"Why did you think we were playing tricks on you, dear?"

Addy shuffled her feet. "Sam said you were."

"That settles it." Hannah shook her head. "I couldn't sleep last night, thinking about this. I knew you'd have a few minutes before your puppet class while Emilie takes dance, so I told everyone to meet here. We need to plan the wedding."

Addy hadn't slept much, either. What had seemed completely reasonable in the heat of anger had glittered like fool's gold in the cold light of dawn. She couldn't force Sam Dawson to marry her. Sleepless hours of brain-twisting turned up one solution. She had to run away. Pack up Emilie, change their names and move somewhere no one, not even a rich slimebag, could ever find them. Looking around the table at the four women who'd befriended her, her throat swelled with tears. "Thank you, but there's not going to be a wedding."

"If it's a question of money, forget it," Belle said breezily. "Cora has plenty of blooms in her garden for your bouquet and the altar. I'll arrange the reception at the hotel, and Phoebe is in charge of invitations and that sort of thing. All you have to do is show up and look beautiful."

The ladies smiled with the satisfaction of plans well-laid.

Addy fought for composure. "No, I can't. You can't."

Four pairs of eyes filled with distress. Phoebe spoke first. "We know you don't want charity, Addy, but what we're discussing isn't charity at all."

"It's our way of thanking you," Hannah added.

"We'd fallen into the trap of feeling sorry for ourselves because we felt old and useless," Belle said. "You came along and bullied us into taking crafts classes and getting involved here at the center. Now, between us, we tutor at the elementary school, teach bridge classes, give cooking lessons, and volunteer at the health clinic. Phoebe even started a ladies' investment club. You showed us we can still be useful and productive even if we have gray hair and a few arthritic twinges.''

''Belle's right, dear. We want to give something back to you.'' Cora's face clouded over. ''I see what it is, dear. Every girl dreams of the wedding she wants. We shouldn't have tried to force our wedding plans on you.''

Embarrassment, gratitude, and the knowledge she didn't deserve their friendship overwhelmed Addy. ''That's not it.'' She forced the words past the painful lump in her throat. ''You're all wonderful, and I know if there was going to be a wedding and you planned it, it would be beautiful, but there isn't going to be a wedding. Sam doesn't want, that is, Sam and I aren't getting married.''

''That's not what you said last night,'' Hannah said.

''I know,'' Addy said distractedly. ''I don't know what I was thinking. Ever since Sam arrived, my whole life has spun out of control. I'm sorry, Hannah, but he drives me crazy.''

''You certainly haven't been the same since Sam blew into town.'' Belle's dark eyes gleamed from behind her rhinestone eyeglass frames. ''Everyone's heard about the yelling match here the other day.'' Her red-lipsticked mouth twitched. ''Hannah told us what happened in your bedroom. My husband Al would have loved painting my nipples pink.''

''Think about the mess, dear,'' Cora frowned. ''If you were in bed, the sheets would be ruined. And rolling about on the floor as Addy and Sam did... We had carpeting in our bedroom.''

Addy turned fiery red. ''Hannah!''

''They wanted to know how you two came to be engaged.''

"I still say what Sam and Addy do in the privacy of their bedrooms is their own business," Phoebe said reprovingly.

"We're not doing anything!" Addy identified with Alice falling down the rabbit's hole.

Eight raised eyebrows wordlessly questioned Addy's statement.

"Don't worry, Addy," Hannah said. "I'll make sure Samuel behaves as a gentleman and marries you."

"No. It was my fault. I made it up about us getting married. I never should have said anything."

Hannah gave Addy a grim smile. "That's sweet of you to take the blame, but not necessary. If Samuel refuses to go through with the wedding, I'll tell him he'll never ever again be allowed to darken my doorstep." Building up steam, she elaborated on her grievance. "The idea. My own grandson seducing my friend in my house and then refusing to make an honest woman of her. I'm so ashamed." She shook her head. "I'll have to call his mother. Jo Jo will be distraught. Samuel may think he's a grown man, but his parents will have something to say about his dastardly behavior, believe you me." Hannah bowed as her three friends rose to their feet and applauded loudly. "I may be old, but I still know the difference between right and wrong."

"Hannah, please," Addy implored. "I don't want to marry Sam."

"Bridal jitters, dear. The night before I married Frank I almost ran away from home." Cora smiled wistfully. "That was so long ago. Sometimes I envy you young girls with a lifetime of love and laughter ahead of you. You're so lucky, dear."

Addy grabbed the roll of paper towel from the table and blew her nose, all the while shaking her head. "Not getting married," she mumbled, and blew again. "Not."

* * *

"You told them what?"

Addy winced at Sam's explosive shout. "You heard me. I said it happened so fast, we decided to wait awhile to see if it was the real thing. You'd go back to Boston, and we'd see if time and distance changed our feelings for each other."

Storm clouds darkened Sam's face. "Mine sure as hell aren't going to change."

"What did you expect me to say? That you're a stupid jerk, and I wouldn't marry a man with your outsized ego and spiteful ways if you held a loaded gun at my head?"

"Does that mean you've had a change of opinion since last night?" Sam asked. "That I can count on you jilting me and breaking my heart?"

"It would serve you right if I did insist you marry me. They had the wedding all planned. You're lucky they hadn't booked the church and mailed out the invitations. When I tried to explain we weren't getting married, they blamed bridal jitters and lovers' quarrels."

"I don't suppose," Sam said coldly, "you bothered to explain the one thing we aren't is lovers."

"Hannah told them about the pink paint." In spite of her resolve, heat painted her face every bit as pink. "And what you were doing with it."

"So to spare everyone's maidenly blushes, you cravenly allowed them to continue in their delusional assumption you and I are what, engaged? I hope you're not expecting me to buy you an expensive engagement ring. Or is a ring you can keep when we have our so-called breakup the price of my freedom? Forget it. I don't trust you, Ms. Johnson. A ring could be another trick to haul me one step closer to the altar." He made two angry circuits of Addy's sitting room before whirling to ask savagely, "Why me? There must be plenty of suckers who don't object to purple walls or being used as an insurance policy.''

"You scared them all away,'' she said acidly.

"The next time,'' he said sourly, "it's every man for himself.'' His eyes narrowed. "Is that why you pulled this trick? Revenge because you think I ruined your chances? Hell, neither Carlson nor Christain had marriage with you on his mind.''

"Hannah and the others disagree with your analysis.''

"What did you expect them to say? That they'd deliberately set you up with ineligible men?''

"There's no reason for them to lie.''

Sam threw his hands in the air. "My grandmother would lie, cheat or steal, and maybe commit mayhem and murder to get me married. But I am not going to marry you.''

"Don't yell at me. If you weren't always kissing me, we wouldn't be engaged now.''

"We are not engaged.'' The blue veins bulging in his neck matched neither his eyes nor his shirt.

"If you want to tell that to your grandmother, be my guest.'' She waited until he had one hand on the doorknob. "Don't be surprised when she hands you your packed suitcase and shows you the front door.''

He turned slowly. "What the hell does that mean?''

"Hannah thinks you've been playing fast and loose with me. Promising me marriage, seducing me, and bailing out when she caught us. When I told her we weren't getting married, she threatened to call your mother.''

"I'm thirty-five years old, Adeline. Even if Grandmother called my mother, what's my mother going to do? Stop my allowance?''

"You still get an allowance?''

"No!" He practically howled. "I do not get an allowance. I was trying to make a point." Sam stalked from the room.

Addy picked up a heart-patterned polymer cane. She'd completed six beads before Sam returned. "Did you manage to weasel out of our engagement?"

"Grandmother's being a little difficult."

Addy studied the six monstrously ugly, misshapen beads on the table before her. "You mean we're still engaged?"

Sam switched tactics, saying in an irritatingly reasonable voice, "Even if we did overlook the fact we have nothing in common, our getting married would never work out. Nobody likes to be used, and you'd be using me to keep Emilie."

Addy smashed a bead with her fist. Sam Dawson annoyed her as no single individual had in her twenty-eight years of life.

"Why did you destroy it?" Sam looked over her shoulder. "I like those. They're the first lovely, refined beads I've seen you make. Small, pastel, ladylike."

Undoubtedly he'd just described the type of woman he preferred. Not that his prejudices regarding the female sex interested Addy the tiniest little bit. She smashed the other five beads.

Sam resumed his pacing. "I had a thought."

"Don't panic. It happens to the rest of us all the time."

He gave her a brief look of disgust. "I'm willing to accept partial responsibility for our predicament."

The phrase "partial responsibility" immediately raised Addy's ire. "I don't know why you refer to our engagement as a predicament." She enjoyed the muscle twitching in his jaw.

Sam halted by the table, and scowled down at her. "I'm willing to make a deal."

"Addy Dawson." She couldn't resist baiting him. "It has a nice sound, don't you think?" She suspected he jammed his hands into his back pockets to keep from strangling her.

"I'm trying to deal with this in a rational manner," he said coolly, "but you would drive a thinking man to drink." When she didn't respond, he said, "You've convinced yourself the only way you can feel secure about retaining custody of Emilie is by getting married. I don't think your custody is a matter of concern, but there's no point in discussing an issue you're emotional about. I'm not going to marry you, but I will help you find a husband."

"Excuse me," Addy said sarcastically, "but I believe we've been down this road before. How dumb do you think I am?"

"Is that a rhetorical question?" He continued. "If you'd bothered to share your concerns with me at the beginning, we could have devised a sensible plan for your future comfort."

"You sound like you're trying to sell me insurance or a cemetery plot."

"If you don't quit interrupting," he said tightly, "you may need both. I'm trying to help you."

"You're trying to escape a marriage noose. While it's tempting to marry you to teach you a lesson, as fond of teaching lessons as you are, I'm not into education at the moment. Quit panicking. I'm going to do what you wanted me to do all along. I'm leaving."

Sam came to an abrupt halt, staring at her from across the room. "Leaving. You're running away?"

"Call it what you like."

"I call it stupid."

"We can't all have Ph.D.'s, Dr. Dawson."

"Where are you going? Where will you live? How do you expect to support yourself?" The questions came with machine-gun rapidity. "You haven't the faintest idea, do you? You're not going anywhere."

"How do you plan to stop me? Lock me in my room?"

"I could. Or I could have you arrested for stealing my grandmother's pearls. I'm sure Carlson will remember those pearls, and how provocatively they nestled between your breasts the other night."

"Hannah loaned me her pearls," Addy said indignantly.

"Your word against hers. Before you claim she'll back you up, let me assure you, she will not."

"Liar."

"Why do you think I allowed my grandmother to insist we continue with this sham of an engagement?"

"Because she threatened to throw you out of her house if you refuse to marry me."

Sam gave her an exasperated look. "Not me. You."

Stunned, Addy slumped against the back of her chair. "Hannah wouldn't... You're lying."

"She has her good name to think of. How long do you think it will take to get all over town she caught you and me having sex on the bedroom floor? How will it look if she condones our activities? Not to mention what will people think when she doesn't fire you from the community center, where, she reminded me, people entrust their children to you. And speaking of children, she only has it on your say-so that Emilie is the daughter of your sister. No one from around here has ever met any sister or any other family member of yours. She's old, she sleeps soundly. Who knows how many men have been climbing the balcony and into your bed at night?"

"She doesn't sleep soundly. She can tell you every time Emilie rolls over at night." Addy hardly knew what she was saying. Her entire brain had gone numb. Shock and disbelief shielded her from the pain she knew she'd suffer later.

"She's also a master manipulator, so wipe that stricken look from your face," Sam said in a harsh voice. "She doesn't believe a word of it. She used that garbage as a threat to keep me in line. She knows I won't dare call her bluff."

"In line? Bluff?" Addy asked in a daze.

"Adeline, hello! Have you been paying any attention at all to what's going on around here? Grandmother brought us together for one reason. Marriage. She's not throwing in the towel until she marches us down the aisle together."

"Since you say Hannah's bluffing, we can ignore our short-lived engagement and the rest is my problem."

"I'm perfectly willing to play chicken with Grandmother when it comes to my life. I'm not willing to gamble with yours and Emilie's. Subject closed."

"It's not closed. Why would Hannah make such a threat?"

"I told you. She wants me to marry you."

"But why?"

"Because, damn it, she likes you!"

"You don't have to shout."

Sam slapped his hands on the table and leaned across the width until his nose practically touched hers. "You'd prefer I paint the words on your chest with pink paint?" he asked through clenched teeth.

"Snarling at me isn't going to solve anything. You're behaving emotionally, not rationally. We need to view the situation calmly and objectively. Apply a little logic."

He slammed the sitting room door so hard the entire house shook. Addy gave him fifteen minutes. He returned in five.

"You're absolutely correct," he said evenly. "Indulging in wishful fantasies at this time solves nothing. We need clear thinking and practical solutions. I have a plan."

"Wishful fantasies?"

"You don't want to know," he said, adding in a surly voice, "since you star in them."

Addy elected not to probe further.

Tossing her a sardonic look, Sam pulled out a chair and sat across the table. "First of all, we need to declare a truce."

"Armed or unarmed?"

"By all means, armed. I'd hate to outlaw that rapier wit of yours. If only you'd use it to cut out your senseless worries about Emilie, we'd all be happier."

Addy thought fast. If she pretended to go along with Sam, he'd think she had changed her mind about running away. She'd play things his way until he left, but as soon as he took flight for Boston, she'd take flight for—for somewhere. "Go ahead," she said meekly. "I'm listening. A truce. OK."

He looked suspiciously at her before saying, "I'm planning to return to Boston next week. Until then, a truce. For a week. Even you ought to be able to keep one for that long."

"Obviously you won't," Addy retorted.

"I'm sorry. It won't happen again." His eyes narrowed, but he chose not to make an issue of Addy's muttering. "You're convinced the answer to your perceived problem is a husband, and a husband does have the virtue of solving my problem." At her look of inquiry, he said with exaggerated patience, "If you're marrying someone else, you can't marry me. The obvious course of action is, I have one week to find you a husband."

"Where do you plan to find this poor sucker?"

"Good question." Picking up some finished beads, he rolled them in his palm. "Maybe we ought to give the ladies' four candidates a second perusal in case I failed to factor in all the necessary data. If none of them work out, there must be more than four single men in this area. If we had more time... There's a couple of men who work for me, a scientist or two I've had contact with, hell, I'd even sacrifice my own brothers."

"The theory being, better your brothers get stuck with bubonic plague than you?"

Sam concentrated on laying the beads one by one in Addy's divided storage tray. "I'm a consultant. I spend more time in planes than I do in my apartment. One day I'm in Philadelphia, the next I'm in Japan. One fellow who works for me is in the middle of being divorced by his wife who decided if she was going to practically be a single parent, she ought to have the dating privileges. Another employee's fiancée dumped him for a college professor. Said she wanted a husband who showed up for dinner every night."

"So for the good of womankind, you're going to stay a bachelor all your life?" Addy asked sarcastically.

"I'd like to get married someday. There are plenty of women who don't want a man continually underfoot." He rolled a bead back and forth in the box with his finger. "Most of them don't want kids underfoot, either, so I guess I'll have to either give up the idea of kids, or maybe switch careers." He switched his gaze to Addy. "I wouldn't be the kind of husband and father you and Emilie want."

Addy came perilously close to asking him what made him so sure. Emilie, at least, would take whatever piece of Sam Dawson she could get. As for Sam... Sam and kids went together like peanut butter and jelly. How sad he couldn't see that. Addy rubbed her elbow. It ached from kneading clay.

Emilie wiggled and squirmed, so excited she couldn't sit still. Addy gave her a quick squeeze. They were waiting for Jim Carlson who had invited them to take the train up Pikes Peak with him and his boys. Jim hadn't mentioned Sam, and Sam hadn't said how he'd arranged the outing. Emilie's anticipation pleased Addy. Regardless of Sam Dawson's instructions, she did not intend to spend the day peering at Jim and his boys under some kind of perverted microscope to see what kind of father and brothers they'd make.

"How much longer, Addy?" Emilie asked impatiently.

"Mr. Carlson will be here soon."

The sound of a throat being cleared came from the other side of the screen. "Carlson just called." Sam opened the screen door. "He can't go. One of his boys has a funny tummy."

Emilie's eyes opened wide. "Can't go?"

"I'm sorry, Emilie. We'll go another time. Mr. Carlson's son won't be sick long. He'll take us another time."

Sam bent his knees to sit beside them on the porch steps. "Actually, he probably won't. When his son got sick at his apartment, Jim called Lois, she went over, and well..." Sam shrugged.

"They're getting back together," Addy guessed. She didn't need Sam's nod for confirmation.

Emilie buried her face in her teddy bear. "I want to ride the train. You said we were. You promised."

"I didn't promise." Holding Emilie's face in her hands, Addy scrunched down to the child's eye level. "I know you want to take the train. If I could make it happen, I would, but I'm not a fairy godmother, Emilie. Riding trains takes money, and I don't have the money right now. At the end of the summer, if I sell enough jewelry, we can ride a train." But not this one.

"Chrissy rode on a plane," Emilie said in a heart-rending voice. "I want to ride on a train."

Emilie's words drew a clear picture for Addy. The treats other children took for granted didn't often come

Emilie's way. Addy swallowed hard. "We will, Sweetheart." Other places had trains. She handed Emilie a tissue from her pocket. "Blow your nose and give me a smile." When Emilie's mouth continued to turn down, Addy put a dark frown on her face. "Addy gets maddy when she doesn't get big smiles." Reluctantly a tremulous smile curved Emilie's mouth. Addy smiled back before giving the little girl a big hug. "I love you, Emilie Johnson. Now go wash the unhappiness from your face."

Emilie ran into the house, banging the screen door behind her. Sam grabbed Addy's ankle when she stood. "You know, I haven't taken that train for years, and I admit I was jealous you and Emilie were going." Still holding her ankle, he stretched out his legs and leaned back on one elbow. "I'll buy Jim's tickets from him and the three of us can go."

Fierce anger surged through Addy's body. Closing her eyes for a moment, she forced herself to breathe slowly and deeply. "I've told you before, Emilie and I don't take charity." She tried to wrest her ankle free.

His grip tightened. "If I showed you some pictures of a woman, by looking at the kind of clothes she wears and so on, could you come up with a necklace designed exclusively for her? The woman I have in mind would be crazy about your stuff. I'd be willing to pay in advance." He hesitated. "I meant to ask you about it earlier."

Addy increased her efforts to break free. She wasn't dumb. The type of woman Sam Dawson escorted wasn't likely to appreciate an Addy Johnson original. Solid gold studded with diamonds would be more appropriate for Sam's Boston beauties. Addy never doubted there was more than one.

Therefore, Sam was offering her charity. Despite claiming he'd meant to ask her earlier, the idea had come to him less than sixty seconds ago when he'd heard

Addy's pathetic sob story to Emilie about how poor they were. He probably couldn't imagine anyone not being able to afford the train ride up Pikes Peak.

Addy hated charity. People offered you charity because they pitied you. It was one thing to accept Sam's help in solving a mutual problem. It was quite another to accept charity. She wasn't about to take one dime from Sam Dawson. "I'm afraid my jewelry is too wild for you."

"A good businesswoman doesn't turn away a customer, Adeline. You'll need the money when you run." Blue eyes blandly noted the look of guilt on Addy's face.

CHAPTER SEVEN

"RUN?" Addy asked nonchalantly after a pause which lasted far too long.

"Do you think I can't tell when someone's humoring me? You figure there's not a chance I'll find you a husband," Sam said, "but you decided it would be easier to bide your time than argue with me. I think you plan to cut and run the minute I leave."

"It's a free country. Think whatever you want."

"I notice you don't tell me I'm wrong."

"I haven't been able to tell you anything since you arrived," Addy retorted.

"That's right, you haven't." Sam stood up and yelled through the screen door. "Emilie, we're taking the train up Pikes Peak today. If you're going, you have one nanosecond to get down here."

"I told you we weren't going with you."

"You can't tell me anything, remember?" Sam laughed at the vexed look on her face. "Don't say it." Turning, he scooped up the child flying through the doorway. "Here's Squirt, raring to go. Grab your stuff, Adeline, we're off to see the Peak."

One look at Emilie's smiles and shining eyes, in stark contrast to her earlier tear-drenched face, told Addy she had no choice. "OK, but I'm paying for Emilie's and my tickets." She'd juggle the budget somehow. She'd hoped to buy Emilie new clothes in a real store before the little girl started kindergarten this fall, but careful shopping at a thrift shop, and if she cut up some of her own clothes for fabric, she could make—

"Are you listening, Adeline? Emilie is my date, so I'm buying her ticket. An independent woman like you can buy your own ticket with the profit you make from selling me a necklace."

Profit without a gallery's cut. Addy's jewelry flew off the shelves, attesting to its popularity. Sam would receive value for his money. "All right. I'll make the jewelry for you."

"Good. I'll scare up some photographs, and you can draw up some ideas and give me an estimate, which I'll pay in advance. If the jewelry ends up costing more, I'll make up the difference," Sam said in a brisk, impersonal voice. "I'm in no rush, say for Christmas?"

"Fine." Addy reached for the screen door. She'd be resettled by then. She'd find a way to send him the necklace.

"And we agree Emilie is my responsibility for the day?"

If Sam Dawson wanted to be in charge of a supercharged four-year old dynamo, who was Addy to object? Her conscience nudged her to warn him. "Emilie can be a handful on a day trip."

"I don't see any problem. You don't suffer from train sickness, do you, Squirt?" Emilie giggled against his neck. "If she has to use the bathroom, I'll find a tree to take her behind."

"There aren't any trees on top. It's above the tree line. You ought to know that."

The corners of Sam's eyes crinkled. "I told Emilie she had one nanosecond to get ready. The same goes for you."

Those who called blue a cold color erred. Some blues surrounded one with warmth and comfort. Sleepy summer afternoon skies. Bluebirds. Worn blue jeans. Teasing blue eyes, one beneath a drooping eyelid. The other beneath a brow raised in silent inquisition.

Addy laughed. Surely she could set aside her worries and her dislike of Sam Dawson for the duration of a train ride up Pikes Peak. For Emilie's sake.

Final preparations required more than a nanosecond, but they soon piled into Addy's old car and headed down Ute Pass toward Manitou Springs, everyone sharing Emilie's infectious good spirits. Where the hillsides weren't covered with a motley array of houses, spikes of pearlescent yucca blooms covered the undulating landscape like candles on a summer green birthday cake. The highway began to twist and sweep between rosy sandstone canyon walls, and a small stream tripped gaily over rocks between the divided lanes of highway. The sun beamed benignly down on them from a sky as blue as Sam's eyes.

"What a gorgeous day. Look at those ice cream scoops of clouds," Addy said.

"Did you bring ice cream?" came a hopeful voice from the backseat.

"What did you bring?" Sam asked. "That tote bag you hauled out weighs more than Squirt."

"I'm mustard, mustard," Emilie chanted before giggling, "Sam calls me Squirt 'cuz I squirt out doors like mustard from bottles."

At least he wasn't calling Emilie Blood Cells. "I brought my lunch," Addy said.

"Don't they serve food on the train?"

Addy widened her eyes in mock horror. "You didn't bring lunch for you and Emilie?"

"I didn't even think about it." After a moment he asked casually, "I don't suppose you brought lunch for us?"

"As I recall, you insisted on taking full responsibility for Emilie today." She headed the car up Ruxton Avenue.

"A bag that large must hold lots of food."

"Not really. Four ham sandwiches, potato chips, three cut up apples, a dozen oatmeal cookies, lemonade, that's all."

"Maybe Emilie could have a crumb or two," Sam said.

"Maybe." Spotting a parking space, Addy swung the car into the crowded parking lot.

"And maybe, if you two don't eat it all, I could have some of the leftovers," Sam said.

"Maybe."

"Will I have to grovel?"

Addy turned off the car. "You betcha." Laughing voices from tourists and the whistling of hummingbirds filled the air.

Suddenly Addy felt as light-headed and carefree as Emilie. She wasn't so young and foolish as to believe her troubles would disappear with a train ride, but the idea of escaping from them for even a few hours made her almost giddy. "Grovel and then some." She unleashed her biggest and brightest smile on Sam.

He made no move to get out of the car, but stared at Addy with the oddest expression on his face.

"It was a joke," Addy said quickly. "I brought plenty to eat for all of us, but if you'd prefer, there's a place to buy food here at the station. Why are you looking at me like that?"

"You don't smile enough. I've never noticed Emilie has your mouth and your smile."

"You were too busy noticing our matching freckles." Addy rolled up the car windows and gathered their things.

Sam pushed the seat out of the way so Emilie could scramble from the car. "Matching freckles, matching mouths, matching hats, but not matching necklaces. Squirt, that's a pretty wild-looking cat. An Adeline Johnson original, I assume."

Emilie turned the pendant over. "My trip necklace."

Sam leaned down to inspect the black markings on the back of the plastic clay oval. "Your name and phone number."

"If I get lost Addy says I hafta show it to a policeman," Emilie said in a self-important voice. "Policeman are nice."

"Very nice." He picked up the heavy tote. "Addy is wise."

"Owls are wise." Emilie skipped alongside Sam, taking two steps to every one of his. "I'm mustard and Addy's a owl."

"Owls look wise," Sam said. "Pigs, however, are extremely intelligent animals."

"Addy's not a pig," Emilie said indignantly, as they waited beside the road to cross over to the railway station.

"What is she?"

Emilie screwed up her face in deep thought. "Grandma Hannah says she's fresh air, but... Addy, what's the mama in my story?"

"A kangaroo? You think I'm a kangaroo?"

"Yes," Emilie said firmly. "Kangaroos like children."

Sam looked down at the child at his side. "What am I?"

"A chocolate cupcake."

Addy laughed at the look of revulsion on Sam's face.

"A chocolate cupcake. Are you saying I'm sweet and gooey?"

Emilie looked at him solemnly. "Chocolate cupcakes are my very favorite thing."

Emilie's answer revealed too much. Addy swallowed hard and leaped in to fill an awkward pause. "You're wrong, Emilie," she said, "Sam is an evil scientist."

"You've learned my secret," he said in a high-pitched cackling voice. "I wander all over the world looking for my favorite food."

"What?" Emilie asked.

"Mustard," he intoned with an evil leer.

Emilie shrieked with laughter, slipping her hand into Sam's larger one as they crossed the busy street.

Addy envied Emilie's uncomplicated approach to life. She didn't care who knew she liked Sam. Remorseful over dragging Emilie into "the paint episode," Addy had explained to her niece she'd said things she didn't mean because she was mad at Sam. Addy wasn't convinced Emilie understood the explanation, but Emilie hadn't seemed overly upset Sam wouldn't be her substitute father. Maybe Emilie didn't understand the concept of having any kind of father at all.

If only Emilie's lack of comprehension continued to insulate the child from reality once she entered school. Children could be cruel to those who differed from them in any way. Addy wished she could give Emilie everything all those other children had. One day she would.

They'd be OK. She'd raised Emilie for almost five years without leaning on anyone. She wouldn't start leaning on a man now, no matter how tempting. She knew he'd soon be walking out of her life, yanking away her supports as he left.

Too many times in the past Addy had painfully rebuilt those supports. At age thirteen when her parents had been killed in a car crash. Through the years when she and Lorie had been shunted from one distant relative to another. Lorie had been the champion support-kicker of all time. Never again would Addy allow anyone to kick away her supports. Not now, when they supported Emilie, too.

Emilie considered herself less Sam's guest than he was her personal toy for the day. Facing the two of them, Addy relaxed against the back of the seat and looked out the window as the train started up the steep rack railway. A creek rushed over boulders alongside the rails, and huge granite rocks rose from yellow patches of sunflowers and cinquefoil mixed with pale lavender wild geranium and scarlet gilia. Aspen fluttered in the shadows of towering pines and blue-tipped spruce trees. A large black and white butterfly flew from a blue columbine.

With one ear Addy listened to the running commentary of the train conductor as he collected tickets; with the other she followed the conversation of Sam and Emilie as he explained the mechanics of cog railroads. Addy doubted Emilie understood one word in twenty of Sam's explanation. The rapt look on Emilie's face had nothing to do with what moved their train up the hill and everything to do with being the focus of Sam's attention. A searing flash of jealousy almost knocked Addy from her seat. She wanted those intense eyes concentrating on her. The crazy admission came as a bolt from the blue.

Dr. Samuel Dawson, Ph.D., was an attractive man. And a dangerous one. Dangerous to Addy. He'd busted into her life with his accusations and scorn and obsession with revenge, and suddenly, inexplicably, vague, restless yearnings wove insidious threads of discontent through her mind and body. A sense of something missing from her life jabbed at her, making her edgy and bad-tempered. Sam confused her by kissing her and smiling at her with those eyes of his. He had to know how potent his baby blues were. A million women had undoubtedly told him so.

"Look! A squirrel!" Emilie bounced on her seat and pointed her sandwich out the window.

"A yellow-bellied marmot," Sam said, embarking on a lesson on the difference between the two small mammals.

On the hillside blue alpine forget-me-nots grew in a cluster. Soon Sam would fly back to Boston. Addy repressed the small knot of tension forming in her stomach.

Emilie would forget Sam in the excitement of moving and starting kindergarten. Addy wondered if she'd be able to forget as easily.

She concentrated on the passing landscape. She'd come to enjoy the view, not to regret what could never be. To the south rose the Sangre de Christo mountain range and the eastern Spanish Peak. In the thin, clear air, they appeared closer than they were. An illusion. Life was full of illusions.

At least one of which a fellow tourist held. "He's good with her, isn't he?"

The voice in her ear turned Addy around.

The elderly woman nodded to Sam crouching beside Emilie atop Pikes Peak inspecting the snow pellets landing on Emilie's jacket sleeve. "I told my kids snow-flakes were Mother Nature shaking her feather beds. I'll bet he's saying something similar."

Addy would bet her last dollar Sam was explaining to Emilie the chemical makeup of snow and why it was snowing on the summit of Pikes Peak in July.

The woman went on. "I like the way fathers today get more involved in raising children. So much better than in the past when a father tended to be a stern-faced man who gave orders and handed down punishments. Your little girl certainly takes after your husband—those blue eyes, but I did notice a few of your freckles on her face." Hearing an impatient middle-aged woman calling her, the woman smiled and said, "My daughter. You and your family have a lovely day today."

"Thank you," Addy managed. "You, too." The woman thought the three of them the quintessential nuclear family. Father, mother and child. Addy stared down the slopes toward Colorado Springs ignoring the tourists around her talking and snapping photographs. A brisk wind chilled her face, bringing the smell of doughnuts. Sam had bought doughnuts for them in the peak top store. Emilie munched hers atop Sam's shoulders as he walked about the peak reading the various signs out loud to Emilie and explaining them. Despite Sam's misgivings, he would make a wonderful father someday for some lucky child. That child wouldn't be Emilie. For Emilie's sake, Addy regretted that fact.

A regret not shared by Sam. "No," he said easily to the older man who sat beside Addy as they traveled back down, "Emilie's not my daughter." Sam smiled down at the child sleeping on his lap before nodding at Addy. "She's her niece."

"She's a cute little tyke." The man had traded seats with his wife so they'd have different views for the descent. He turned to Addy. "It's nice of you and your husband to bring her along."

"We're not married," Sam and Addy said in unison.

The man shook his head. "You modern generation. I suppose you're 'POOSLT's or 'SPLT's or whatever they call it these days when two people live together without bothering to get married."

Addy's face turned crimson. "We don't live together," she said quickly. "Sam's in town visiting his grandmother."

The man snorted. "Where would you kids be if my generation hadn't married and had kids?" He ignored his wife hushing him from across the aisle. "Mary and I been married fifty-one years, got four kids and ten grandkids. We believe in marriage."

"Then you're the gentleman to convince Addy she needs to get married. She's raising her niece, and I'm sure you agree, sir, a child needs a father."

"Why won't you marry him?" The man looked at Addy.

She could have happily pushed Sam from the train. Instead she lowered her eyelashes and said primly, "He turned down my proposal."

Sam laughed, not the least bit disconcerted. "We agree we wouldn't suit. She'll be marrying someone else, as soon as we agree on whom she should marry. You've been married long enough to be somewhat of an authority on marriage. What traits and qualifications do you think we ought to look for in a life-long partner for Addy and a father for Emilie?"

If Sam had offered the man a million dollars, he couldn't have made him happier. "First of all..." The man was off and running.

Shifting Emilie on his lap, Sam pulled out a small notebook and pen and started taking notes. Soon the man's wife joined the conversation, then the five people sitting in her section of seats contributed. By the time the little train pulled into the gaily-colored station, Sam had canvassed the entire railroad car, soliciting advice and opinions. Emilie awakened in Addy's lap.

"I think you got a little carried away asking the conductor if you could use his microphone," Addy said, still outraged minutes later as they climbed into her ovenlike car.

"There's no such thing as having too much information," Sam dismissed her indignation. "As scientific studies go, that wasn't the most accurate, but I acquired a wealth of empirical data. Once I transcribe my notes and chart the data, we'll have the personality profile of your perfect husband. From there it's just a matter of laying the profile over the available bachelors, and then..." Loudly he hummed wedding music by Lohengrin.

Addy wished she hadn't eaten a third doughnut on the summit. It caused a sick feeling in the pit of her stomach.

Addy saw the letter the instant she entered the shadowed hall. Hannah had placed it in a silver toast rack on the small table. Sam and Emilie, proclaiming starvation, headed toward the kitchen. Reluctantly picking up the letter, Addy dragged her heavy legs up the stairs to the privacy of her room. She slit open the envelope with trembling fingers, staring vacantly at the small red dot of blood which welled up where the paper sliced through her skin.

Lorie's former lawyer had mailed the letter to Addy without comment. Addy quickly scanned the words, then forced herself to read the letter slowly. The second reading produced no relief.

"Addy, Addy!" Emilie's high-pitched voice hollered stridently up the stairs. "Come see."

"All right. I'm coming." She carefully folded the letter into small squares and slid it into the pocket of her purple skirt.

Sam and Emilie sat at the table in the kitchen. Jelly dripped in huge amethyst glops from the sandwich Sam ate.

"I made the sandwiches," Emilie said proudly. "Sam made the glasses of milk."

A plate with two folded-over slices of bread sat waiting for Addy. "That's nice," Addy said absently, her hand crushing the letter in her pocket. She sat at the table, phrases from the letter assaulting her.

After a while, Sam asked, "Something wrong with your sandwich?"

"What? Oh, no. It's delicious."

"Then why aren't you eating it?"

"I am." She followed the direction of Sam's gaze to her plate. Tiny pieces of sandwich had been smashed into a solid heap on her plate. Peanut butter and jelly coated her fingers. "I guess I'm not very hungry."

Sam raised an eyebrow, but made no comment, confining his conversation to a discussion with Emilie about their train trip.

Addy had to think, to make plans. Her thoughts Ping-Ponged around her brain, to return again and again to a single overriding conviction. She had to pack up Emilie and get her away before this monster came to take her niece away.

With the decision made, a small measure of peace settled over Addy. Not everyone would agree with her decision, but running beat waiting. Waiting equated to surrendering. Addy looked around. Sam and Emilie no longer sat across from her.

Sam walked into the kitchen. "Emilie is with Grandmother. OK, what's the problem?"

"Nothing. No problem. Everything's fine. Why do you ask?" Instead of answering he eyed her plate. Addy looked down. She'd made little balls from her smashed sandwich and was rolling them around on her plate. She snatched up her napkin and carefully wiped off her fingers. "I'm fine," she repeated. Her assurance wouldn't fool a two-year-old.

Sam leaned back in the chair across the table. "Meta-stable," he pronounced.

Addy gave him a blank look.

"It's a chemistry word for a state of being neither stable nor unstable, which means it can become more of one or the other. In your case, you look as if you're close to becoming totally unstable. About to disinte-grate, in fact. So don't weave me any tales of you being fine. You're clearly not fine, so what happened between the time we walked in the door and you came down for a snack?" His gaze sharpened. "The mail. You picked up a letter. Another one from your anonymous correspondent?"

Wordlessly Addy drew the creased letter from her pocket and held it out.

Sam smoothed out the paper. "'Dear Ms. Johnson.'" He gave a start of surprise. "This one's written to you, not your sister's lawyer. Did your anonymous correspondent mail it direct?''

"No.'' But the letter writer was closing in on her.

Sam resumed reading the letter out loud. '' 'I assume your sister's lawyer has forwarded to you the other two letters I wrote seeking information on the child borne by Ms. Loraine Johnson, fathered by William R. Burgess Jr. When I received no response to those letters, I set about making my own inquiries. Acting on information I believed to be accurate, I hired a private detective to search hospital records in the state of Colorado for any record of the child.' ''

"A friend of Lorie's wouldn't have gone to that expense and trouble." To Addy's amazement, her voice worked. "Keep reading."

'' 'I have now learned a Loraine Johnson gave birth to a baby daughter named Emilie Adeline on August 30, 1992, in Denver. Her birth certificate listed the father as Unknown. I am assuming this child is the child I am seeking information about.'

'' 'Further search led the detective to the apartment where you lived at the time Emilie was born. A photograph of Loraine shown to your neighbors elicited the information that you and the child moved away after your sister's death. The neighbors were unable to tell the detective where you relocated, but it is only a matter of time before the detective finds you.' '' Sam looked up from the wrinkled page. "Why did you move? To elude pursuit?"

"No. It never occurred to me... I never thought to tell anyone not to say anything. I never imagined he'd come looking for us. I moved because—'' she twisted her hands in her lap ''—too many unhappy memories. I wanted Emilie to grow up in a happy place. Since then we've moved several times... Rent increases, one place the owners sold, a better neighborhood for Emilie to play in . . ." Almost to herself she added, "I didn't think to hide, even so, it'll take a while to find us."

Sam started to say something, stopped, then turned his attention back to the letter. He read silently, but the words were burned on Addy's brain.

"'It has become a matter of some urgency for me to locate the child and learn the circumstances of her current situation and satisfy myself as to her well-being. I would be happy to meet with you and your husband, if you now have one, at a time and place of your choosing. I am more than willing to fly to Colorado on a moment's notice. I am anxious to meet the people raising Emilie and, of course, to see Emilie for myself. As I mentioned before, I would like to discuss with you issues concerning the child. I assure you it would be in your and Emilie's best interests to agree to such a meeting. I shall look forward to hearing from you in the near future. Sincerely, William Burgess.'"

Addy could sit no longer. Jumping to her feet, she paced back and forth across the small expanse of kitchen floor. "The despicable, villainous louse. A 'personal interest in Emilie.' Who does he think he is? After all these years, thinking he can have her."

"Maybe he wants to reassure himself she's doing well. He says nothing more than he wants to meet her."

"Don't you understand?" Addy practically shouted. "He's a spoiler. He plans to challenge my custody of her. I won't let him. He can't have her. How dare he?" She shoved a chair out of her path. "Where was he when she needed middle-of-the-night feedings? Where was he when her mother abandoned us? Where was he when she was sick and needed rocking for hours? He was out in Hollywood seducing more starlets, that's where he was. And now he's threatening me. It's not enough he killed Lorie, he wants to destroy her daughter. I won't let him. Do you hear me? I will not let him."

"You don't know—"

"Don't you dare—" Addy whirled "—tell me what I do and don't know. I know. He's evil. Ruining an innocent young girl, making her someone I didn't know. Someone hard, cruel, ugly..." Turning from him, she stuffed her fist in her mouth, biting down hard on her knuckles.

A wooden chair crashed to the linoleum behind her, and Sam's hands fell heavily to her shoulders. "C'mon, Adeline, pull yourself together—"

"That's what I said." The harsh laugh tore her throat. She welcomed the pain. "'Pull yourself together, Lorie,' I said. 'It's only two years.' There wasn't enough money. Our folks didn't have much insurance. Our relatives were all kind, but we were burdens on them, and we knew it. They passed us around—spreading the burden, Aunt Marie once said, not knowing I heard."

"I don't understand what—"

"If I didn't go to the university then, I lost the scholarship. I couldn't risk not getting another one. She was sixteen. Two years. I thought it would be OK. Only it wasn't. She was too pretty. The boys liked her too much, the girls not enough. She didn't realize what was happening until it was too late. Boys took her out to park, but they took other girls, more respectable girls, to dances. She had no friends. We'd moved too often. All she had was me. And all I could think about was going off to college."

"You can't blame yourself."

"She cried and begged me not to leave her. I told her to pull herself together. Two years later I begged her to come to the university. She had no scholarship—her grades had plummeted—but I thought if we both held down jobs while we went to school, and got some loans... She looked me right in the eye and said since I'd wanted to go off to school so badly without her, I could stay at school without her."

"That's when she went to Hollywood?"

"I don't even know where she got the money for the bus ride out there," Addy said tonelessly. She didn't want to know. After Lorie left, her aunt's husband dropped some angry hints about blackmail to Addy. After that vacation, Addy never visited that particular aunt and uncle again. She suspected her decision to stay away relieved them. Future annual Christmas cards from her aunt never mentioned Lorie.

Addy's eyelids rubbed her eyes with sandpaper. "She thought I cared less about her than going to school. Isn't that crazy?" She couldn't cry. She'd used up her quota of tears for Lorie years ago. "I loved her more than anything. I thought I was thinking about our future."

"You were."

"I convinced myself I was. Because I wanted to go to college. I wanted to get away from being an object of charity. My selfishness killed my sister. I shouldn't have left her. I'm sure I could have gotten another scholarship, a loan, something... If I had stayed she wouldn't have started on her destructive spiral downward."

"What happened wasn't your fault."

Addy twisted out of his grasp, and faced him, dry-eyed. "You haven't been listening. I murdered my sister. If I'd held a gun to her head and pulled the trigger, I couldn't have killed her deader than I did by walking out on her."

"Adeline, you can't—"

"I will never, ever walk away from Emilie. Never. If I have to lie, steal, cheat ..."

"Or marry."

Addy looked him squarely in the eye. "Or marry."

"All right. Marry me."

CHAPTER EIGHT

A STARK silence filled the kitchen, broken only by the loud ticking of the wall clock. Addy stared dumbfounded at Sam. His entire body appeared carved from stone. Only the shock in his eyes betrayed him. The marriage proposal had stunned him as much as it had stunned Addy. Thanks to her pathetic confession, Sam Dawson had, undoubtedly for the first time in his life, spoken without thinking.

Sam blinked, and the shock disappeared from his eyes, so quickly and completely Addy might have imagined it. Except she hadn't. The cool blue gaze locked on her face as Sam waited for her answer told her more clearly than words that, having made the marriage proposal, Sam considered himself bound to honor it.

If she said yes, he'd marry her. Emilie would have a father. Addy could pretend she didn't know the prospect of marriage to her horrified Sam. Maybe he really did want to marry her. She couldn't jeopardize Emilie's future because of one fleeting emotion she may or may not have seen in Sam's eyes. There was only one way to find out. "Why did you say that? About me marrying you?"

"Adeline, ever since I arrived in Colorado, you've been obsessing over the need to acquire a husband," he said with exaggerated patience. "How many other available men do you know?"

His question answered hers. Pity, and nothing else, had prompted his proposal. Besides, he was hardly available. "What about your Boston beauty?"

"There is no Boston beauty."

139

"You lied about that? Darn you." She wanted to slug him. "I knew you made it up. I knew it. It was charity." Just like his involuntary marriage proposal. Resuming her pacing, she showed massive restraint in kicking a table leg in passing instead of kicking Sam. "I hate charity." She shoved a chair out of her path. "Hate it, hate it, hate it."

"Do you think you could stop with the temper tantrum and tell me what you are talking about?"

"The mythical woman you supposedly wanted me to design a necklace for." She could hardly tell him she was talking about stupid ignoramuses who offered marriage out of pity before they even realized what they were saying. Pity! She didn't want his stupid pity.

Dawning comprehension supplanted the puzzled look on Sam's face. "She's not from Boston, that is—"

"The point is not where she lives." Addy wanted to sit down and howl. "But that she exists."

Sam gave her a startled look. "Does she matter?"

"Of course she matters, you idiot." Everything mattered. Nothing mattered. "If you're committed to her..." Addy grabbed the dirty plates from the table and flung them into the dishwasher. Peanut butter stuck to her fingers. Peanut butter. Blast peanut butter. The dishwasher would never remove the peanut butter. She hated peanut butter. She grabbed the dishes from the dishwasher and scrubbed and scrubbed the surface of the plates. If she had her way peanut butter would be banished from the face of the earth. His Boston beauty, who wasn't from Boston, undoubtedly never had peanut butter in her fancy condo which certainly wouldn't have purple walls. Nor would she have kids around who thought there was only one major food group—peanut butter and its by-products such as peanut butter cookies.

Sam rescued the plates and stuck them in the dishwasher. "No woman, from Boston or anywhere else, expects me to propose marriage to her. No hearts will break when we get married."

"You never wanted jewelry. Now I owe you for the train ticket. Lying to me about wanting a necklace was the same as stealing money from my purse." Focusing on the jewelry kept her thoughts from other, immensely more painful subjects.

"You're overwrought. Calm down so we can discuss this in a calm and reasonable manner."

"I'm not overwrought," Addy screeched, "I'm not wrought at all. I am going to kill you, but I am not overwrought. I should have known. I did know. You don't even like my jewelry. Why would you want your girlfriend to wear it?"

Sam sighed. "Fine. We'll deal first with the issue of the jewelry. I want you to make me a necklace. I commissioned it, and I will pay you for it, even though you're going to be my wife. Let me finish," he said as she opened her mouth. "As for my like or dislike of your jewelry, my tastes are irrelevant. The women of my acquaintance dress to please themselves."

"Considering the way you've criticized every stitch on my body from the moment you walked in Hannah's front door, I find it hard to believe any woman within a hundred-mile radius of you wears anything but lab coats or beige."

"This particular woman wears black night and day."

"She sleeps in black?"

"Since she doesn't wear jewelry to bed, what difference does it make to you what she sleeps in?"

"None," Addy snapped.

"Then quit probing for information on my sex life," he said mildly. "We're not married yet."

Addy knew her face matched her crimson blouse. "I haven't the slightest bit of interest in your sex life, and I'm not going to marry you. My sole interest in her clothing is to help me personalize her jewelry."

"She always wears plain black clothes and huge jewelry. Her necklaces, collected from all over the world, include pearls and gemstones and beads made from about anything you can think of, and more you never thought of. The more exotic, the better." Sam gave her a mocking look. "Anything else you want to know? Her favorite breakfast is a banana and peanut butter sandwich, and she likes it served in bed."

"I'm sure that will be sufficient." He knew what she wore to bed. He knew what she ate for breakfast. He spent nights with her. In her bed.

"There is one more thing, Adeline. The woman I want the necklace for is my mother. Now," he asked politely, "can we move on to the more important subject of our marriage?"

"No." He really expected her to believe he wanted a necklace for his mother?

He sighed again. "What else is there to discuss about the jewelry?"

"I meant, no, I'm not going to marry you." He'd probably give the necklace to the woman as a farewell gift. Or maybe he had no intention of bidding the woman farewell. It wasn't as if he'd be marrying Addy because he was crazy in love with her.

"Adeline, I was lured out here to marry—"

"I had nothing to do with that letter. I never wanted to marry you. I don't want to marry you. I'm not going to marry you."

"Why not?"

"Because I don't want to. What are you, some kind of god that a woman dare not reject your marriage proposal, no matter how..." She couldn't find the word she wanted. "Awful it is?"

"Excuse me," he said sarcastically, "I didn't realize the moment called for champagne and red roses and me down on my knees. I thought I was offering you a helping hand."

A helping hand. As opposed to seeking her hand in marriage. Addy clenched the top of the nearest chair. He meant charity. She looked at the chair, then at Sam. With his height, the weight of the massive chair, not to mention she couldn't count on him to stand passively by while she hefted the furniture over her head... Reluctantly she concluded she'd never be able to break the chair over his head. She never considered the chair might break his thick skull. The bulldog look on his face told her he wouldn't accept another rejection of his suggestion—she refused to call it a proposal. Addy temporized. "This letter, your offer...everything has messed up my mind." That part was true. "I need time to think." Also true. "I'll let you know my decision later." Maybe not so true.

Sam scrutinized her face. "Is your reluctance based on a belief I have another woman somewhere?"

"No." She would have turned him down anyway.

"As you've repeatedly pointed out, I'm not the best catch in the western hemisphere, but I think we could work things out."

He sounded so sincere. Addy could almost believe he'd managed to convince himself he wouldn't mind marrying her. Almost. "As long as we have white living rooms and beige furniture and I allow you to select my clothes?" As if that was the issue.

He frowned. "Do you really think—"

"No." He'd spoken so precipitously he wouldn't have considered any of the ramifications of marriage. He no doubt planned to marry Addy, give Emilie a father in name and then return to Boston where he'd never to have to deal with Addy or Emilie again.

"You're concerned I won't make a good father for Emilie. That's it, isn't it?" he asked heavily.

Addy stared at him in astonishment. He'd make Emilie a wonderful father. Even if he was so stupid he didn't understand anything about anything. "Don't be ridiculous,'' she snapped. ''I just need time to think about it. To analyze the data. In a calm and reasonable manner.'' She fled the kitchen for the security of her rooms, barreling up the stairs and through the sitting room doorway.

Hannah grabbed the top of the stepladder she stood on. ''Goodness, Addy, you took ten years from my life.'' Reaching back up, she removed Addy's grandmother's wedding dress from where it hung on the sitting room wall and carefully handed the dress down to a waiting Emilie.

Addy skidded to a halt. ''What are you doing?''

''Getting down your wedding dress. We may need to do a little altering, and it could use freshening up.''

Emilie, conscious of the enormous responsibility resting on her shoulders, took careful mincing steps to the sofa where she gingerly laid down the dress. She immediately whirled and ran to Addy's side. ''Aunt Cora said I get to carry pink roses.''

Addy helped Hannah down from the stepladder. ''Pink roses?''

''For our wedding.'' Emilie dashed back to the sofa and softly stroked the yellowed white satin. ''We're gonna marry Sam, Addy. Aren't you glad?''

A number of emotions rocked Addy. Gladness didn't happen to be one of them.

Seated in Hannah's front parlor, the four women smiled and looked expectantly at Addy when she came in after putting Emilie to bed. Addy took a deep breath and plunged ahead. ''Hannah told me you were coming over this evening to discuss wedding plans.'' All smiles widened as they nodded. ''Don't you remember my telling you we don't plan to get married for a while? That we're going to see how things go after Sam returns to Boston?'' Addy intended to nip this wedding business in the bud.

"Yes, dear, but that was before you had to get married."

"Had to get married?" Addy asked. "Cora, I don't have to get married."

"No shame in it," Phoebe said. "Mr. Carlson, Jim's father, counseled young mothers to marry for the sake of the baby."

Addy turned to the retired legal secretary. "Shame? Baby? I'm not expecting a baby."

Belle laughed. "Of course not. Hannah said Emilie's father threatened to take Emilie away if you're not married, so Sam offered to marry you. We've always said Emilie needed a father."

"You don't have to worry about what kind of father Sam will make Emilie. I'm a little prejudiced about my grandchildren, but Sam's the oldest and he always watched out for his two younger brothers. What scamps they were," Hannah added fondly.

"He'll be a wonderful father, but I'm not sure—"

"Of course not, dear. Marriage is a big step and it's hard to be sure, but love smooths the way."

Addy's throat constricted. Love had nothing to do with anything. It certainly had nothing to do with her and Sam. At least, it had nothing to do with Sam. And where had that particular clarification come from? "Things aren't quite what you think. The man hasn't actually made any overt threats. I don't know yet what I'm going to do, and—"

"You do what Sam says, dear."

"I have no intention of doing something just because Samuel Dawson tells me to."

"Good for you," Hannah said briskly. "Sam has a tendency to be kind of bossy. Comes from being the oldest child. Don't you let him pull that nonsense on you. Now," his bossy grandmother said, "Sam has to be back in Boston Monday, so the wedding will be late Saturday afternoon. I wanted a morning wedding but the chapel was booked. You won't be able to have a honeymoon, but you can at least spend Saturday night in a bridal suite."

"I don't believe this," Addy muttered. They were all getting senile. If she humored them, she'd end up walking down the aisle in her grandmother's wedding dress. A dress, hanging at this very minute on the kitchen porch drying after Hannah had hand-washed it in the large pantry sink.

"I know," Cora beamed, "love can turn your life topsy-turvy. Only this morning when I was walking in my garden I told Sweetie Pie—my kitty cat, dear—it's Kismet."

"Sam and I?" Addy had lost complete control of the conversation. No. Lost implied she'd once had control.

"No, dear. My roses. I've never seen them so beautiful. As if they knew they had to look their best for your wedding."

She'd wandered into an insane asylum. Desperately Addy sought words to stem the relentless tide sweeping her toward the altar.

Phoebe looked at her list. "I called May from the children's shop—she comes into the law firm now and then, business leases and so on. She has at least three dresses which she says will be perfect. I'm meeting her at the shop tomorrow, and I'll bring the dresses by so Emilie can pick her favorite. Sam can take care of the wedding rings."

"How do you feel about caviar, Addy?" Belle asked. "I've never liked it myself, but if you do...?"

"I've never had it." They'd replaced her brain with cobwebs.

"Maybe we should serve it," Belle said thoughtfully. "Isn't it one of those foods that drive men wild? Anything ovoid?"

"Isn't caviar round, dear? Oysters are what you want."

"Raw?" Phoebe asked with interest. "Or cooked and served with butter and garlic?"

"I think butter and garlic are for snails," Hannah said. "We don't want anything with garlic."

"I'll ask John Christain. He'll know," Belle said.

Addy ran from the room. To her credit, she didn't run screaming.

Sam sat in the back parlor intent on the computer screen in front of him.

"You've got to stop them," Addy gasped. "Roses with Kismet and Emilie buying dresses and whether you eat snails or oysters with garlic. They've gone berserk. You have to stop them."

"Just a sec. Let me finish reading my E-mail."

"E-mail! Forget your E-mail. This is an emergency." Addy leaned down to punch some buttons, any buttons to turn off his blasted computer.

Sam grabbed her hands. "Emilie OK?" At her nod, his muscles relaxed. "Be with you in a minute." His gaze returned to the screen, and his grasp of Addy's hands loosened.

She spied a cord and reached over to yank it loose from whatever it was attached to. Her fingers almost had it when Sam sensed her motion, and suddenly she had his complete attention. Steel arms slung her away from her goal and deposited her on Sam's hard thighs. His muscles flexed beneath her as, with a hard thrust of his legs, he shoved the heavy old wheeled office chair of his grandfather's away from the library table he used as a desk. Penetrating blue eyes glared at her from inches away. "What the hell is wrong with you? Oysters and roses? Who's going berserk?"

"Them! They're planning our wedding!"

"If you don't want oysters and roses, say so," Sam said in a reasonable voice. "It's your wedding."

"It's not my wedding!"

"Whose wedding are they planning?"

"Mine! Aren't you listening?"

Sam's eyes narrowed, and he cupped a hand around her cheek. "Your skin feels warm. I wonder if you got too much sun today."

"No!"

"I hope you're not coming down with some kind of bug. I'd hate to have you miss your own wedding. Women are supposed to like the fuss, the dress, the flowers and all that. A justice of the peace would have suited me, but Grandmother said it wouldn't be fair to you."

Addy froze. "You know they're in there planning the wedding?" At his nod, she said carefully, "I thought I told you I wanted to think about your offer."

"In a calm and reasonable manner, you said." The arm around her waist slackened and slid down until his hand rested against her hip. "I knew after you studied all the data, you'd reach the same inevitable conclusion I reached. You'd agree to marry me."

His hand burned her skin through her caftan. "Why would I do that?" She should throw the old teal blue garment away. The fabric had worn too thin. She tried to edge away from his hand.

Sam's hand tightened, and he shifted his legs, sliding her closer to the trunk of his body. "It's a question of resources. Faced with a limited amount of time and limited amount of eligible men, there is no one but me." He ran his finger along the edge of her neckline. "I don't care whether or not you wear beige, but I've been thinking about that lab coat."

"Lab coat?" She wanted to argue his conclusion about marrying him, but her mind refused to consider anything but the finger heating her skin.

He slid brightly-colored fabric over her shoulder and down her arm. "I don't spend all my time thinking about test tubes or computers or venture capital." Amusement warmed his voice.

"I never said you did." Every hair on her arm quivered with electricity. "What's that have to do with lab coats?"

"I've been sitting here since dinner trying to work. I look at the computer and instead of seeing grafts and charts, I see me coming home and you sitting at the table working on your jewelry and you turn around and stand up and you're wearing a white lab coat. A short lab coat. And nothing else." Sam loosened her neckline until the caftan slid down both shoulders.

"I hardly ever wear white." Addy feared breathing, afraid the slightest movement might dislodge the material from its tenuous perch on the taut tips of her breasts.

Sam gave her a slow wicked smile, taking pleasure in her dilemma. Leaning closer, he slowly brushed her mouth with his tongue. Addy parted her lips and half sighed and half shivered. The soft teal cotton slithered to her waist. A breeze from the overhead fan caressed her bare breasts.

"Belle wondered if you wanted champagne and Cora wanted to ask if you cared what color of roses she selected, but perhaps this isn't a good time." The bright, unexpected voice belonged to Hannah.

Sam pressed Addy against his chest and pulled up her caftan, covering her bare back. "No, Grandmother," he said levelly, "I don't think this is a good time."

Addy had never considered herself as having masochistic tendencies, but nothing could have kept her from raising her head from Sam's shoulder and looking toward the doorway. Hannah beamed back at her. Addy wanted to weep.

Sam waited until his grandmother disappeared down the hallway before he spoke. "I'm sorry. The next time I'll remember to shut and lock the door."

Addy considered telling him there would be no next time, but nothing she said in this house seemed to be heard. Gathering herself together, she stood up. Sam made no move to stop her. Why would he? He needed white lab coats for inspiration. The open doorway promised at least temporary escape.

"Addy, there is no other option." Compassion and something else—regret?—tinged Sam's voice.

Not bothering to respond, Addy walked from the room, closing the door behind her. She hated to think what might have happened if she'd closed the door behind her when she'd gone into the room. She hadn't exactly been fighting Sam off.

The satisfied look on Hannah's face swam across her vision. Being caught half naked in Sam's embrace for a second time dynamited any possibility of convincing the ladies she and Sam were not getting married. Which they weren't. She knew that now. Not on Saturday afternoon or any other time.

Pain mounted in Addy's head. She couldn't marry Sam and she couldn't stay here. More than ever, she had to run. Even if her and Emilie's future together wasn't threatened by that slime from California, she couldn't stay here. Not after the peep show she and Sam had put on for Hannah. Addy squeezed her eyes shut in painful remembrance of Hannah's threats voiced to Sam. Sam said Hannah hadn't meant them, but people didn't want their children taught by immoral women. As John Christain said, this was a small town and gossip thrived.

John Christain. A plan began taking shape in Addy's mind. A desperate plan. Sam claimed a demonstration was worth a thousand words or something like that. Addy'd always thought that applied to pictures, but she understood the underlying principle. First she had to stop this wedding business; then she and Emilie would run.

A variation on her plan suggested itself. If the slime could be tricked, a red herring of some sort, causing him to look in the wrong place. Such as Boston. She'd need to plan skillfully.

Sitting at her worktable, Addy looked at the clay cane she'd started before dinner. Sam Dawson would have his necklace before she left. The sketch she used to build the cane almost brought a smile to her face. Let him explain this to his Boston beauty who wasn't from Boston. His mother. Addy snorted loudly. The crude sound did little to ease her heart ache. Her hand hovered over her small kneaded mounds of polymer clay as she selected her choices of colors for the cane.

Choices. Paths chosen or not chosen. Choices made by her. Choices taken from her. Choices. The very word made her ill. She remembered screaming at the minister by the grave site after her parents' funeral. Why were her parents chosen to die? The minister had looked down his nose at her and told her it wasn't her place to ask why such things happened. One of her aunts had dragged Addy away, Addy screaming angrily at him all the way to the car that she was their daughter so it was her place.

From that day, her choices were made by others. Where she lived, where she went to school, what she ate, what she wore. Kind, well-meaning others, but others all the same.

The first real choice she'd made on her own had been to leave Lorie and go off to college. A disastrous landmark in choices.

This time she'd choose better. She kneaded pale pinkish-ivory for the figure's body. The color used to be called flesh before people in charge of such things woke up to the belated recognition that flesh came in a multitude of colors. The color of Sam's finger against her skin.

Addy squeezed clay in each hand. Sam. Emilie. Choices. At first glance, marrying Sam for Emilie's sake appeared a no-brainer choice. Addy slumped in her chair. First glances could be deceptive. Yes, Sam would be a great father, and yes, the thought of them marrying Sam thrilled Emilie. How long before the thrill wore off? How long before Emilie questioned why Sam had married Addy when his heart belonged to another woman? At what age would Emilie suspect Sam had sacrificed for her? Such a sacrifice would be an incredible burden for a young woman to carry.

And Sam. How long before he regretted his generosity? How long before he tried to mold Addy into someone she wasn't and didn't want to be? A man like Sam wanted classic, uncluttered rooms. Barren rooms. He didn't want the comfortable chaos and remnants of the past which Addy thought enriched Emilie's life. Junk, he called it, and he didn't want it.

A single tear burned a trail down Addy's cheek. He didn't want her. She didn't blame him. Who would want a wildly dressed woman who lived in purple and pink rooms and who'd stupidly fallen in love with the wrong man? Just because Hannah and her friends thought Sam walked on water; just because Emilie adored him; just because he was smart and funny and generous; just because when he kissed Addy her entire body tingled and the world went bright and all things seemed possible.

At age twenty-eight, Adeline Johnson knew all things weren't possible. It wasn't possible to marry Sam Dawson. Not when the groom was motived by a sense of chivalry, and he thought the bride was motived by need. Not when the bride had fallen head-over-heels in love with the groom. Loving Sam, she couldn't tie him to her for all the wrong reasons. She had to set him free. She could only hope her choice would ultimately prove to be the right choice for Emilie. Putting down the clay, Addy went in search of the phone directory and John Christain's phone number.

"I never thought I was a coward at heart, but I have to admit I'm having second, third and tenth thoughts," John Christain said.

Addy gave him the same glazed smile she'd given him the last million or so times he'd repeated his misgivings since he arrived twenty minutes ago. Curbing her irritation, she patiently repeated, "Everything will be fine. Sam Dawson's not the type to throw punches. If he's annoyed with anyone, it will be me."

"Tell me again why we're doing this, and why I let you talk me into it." John's testy voice gave evidence of a definitely thinning veneer of suave amiability.

"You're doing it because at first you thought it sounded amusing. Then, when you chickened out, I threatened you. If you don't do it, I'll smear peanut butter and shaving cream and shoe polish all over your car."

"I knew it wasn't out of the goodness of my heart." He shuddered. "Do you have any idea what those could do to the finish?"

Addy hadn't the faintest idea, but apparently the threat had been inspired.

John's eyes narrowed suspiciously. "This isn't a trick to get me to marry you, is it?"

"No, John." Addy sighed. "If I wanted to get married, I could marry Sam and we wouldn't have to go through with this charade."

"Why don't you marry him? The whole town knows there's a big wedding planned for tomorrow."

"Call me picky, but I think a bride should be consulted on a few things about her wedding."

"You mean to tell me your nose is out of joint because they didn't check with you before ordering oysters and champagne?"

His question immediately diverted Addy. "You're kidding. They're having oysters? Did Belle really ask you which foods are supposed to be... Never mind." Hastily Addy yanked herself back to her grievance. "I mean brides like to be consulted about the identity of their grooms."

"Let me get this straight. Sam Dawson never asked you to marry him, but his grandmother and Belle Rater and the other ladies are planning to marry you off to him?"

"Of course he asked me to marry him," Addy said impatiently. Did Belle know what a total moron John Christain was?

"Lady, one of us is badly confused."

"It's not me," Addy retorted. "Just do what I told you and everything will be fine." Not exactly fine, but definitely over. "Emilie is at a friend's house, and Sam went to run errands and he's picking up Hannah at Cora's house on his way back." Addy glanced at the wall clock. "They should be back any minute now. Did you park your car right in front like I told you, so they see it first thing?"

"I hope it doesn't slide down the hill. Maybe I better go move—"

"Too late. I heard car doors and that's Sam's voice. Hurry. Over here on the sofa."

Knuckles tattooing on the door preceded Sam's stroll into Addy's sitting room. "Adeline..." Whatever he was going to say died unsaid.

Trailing her fingers down John's bare back beneath his unbuttoned shirt, Addy looked over John's shoulder and gazed at Sam's ear. "First you knock, then you wait until someone tells you to come in, then you open the door and walk in."

"Addy Johnson!"

Addy's stomach plummeted as she saw Hannah's shocked face peering around Sam's broad shoulders.

"I'll handle this." Gently maneuvering his grandmother back into the hallway, Sam firmly closed the door. "Well, Adeline?"

"Well, Adeline?" she echoed mockingly. "You said the other day your sex life was no business of mine since we weren't married." She shoved her elbow into John's ribcage. He finally came out of his state of torpor and raised himself from where he lay sprawled across Addy's reclining body. Ignoring John as he hastily buttoned his shirt and tucked it into his unbuttoned trousers waistband, Addy sat up slowly. Deliberately she left her purple blouse hanging open over her lacy red camisole. "I should have remembered your caution about locking doors."

"I said we weren't married yet." He emphasized the last word. "I suggested locking the doors to protect you and I. Not you and him." Sam didn't even glance at John.

"Maybe now's not the best time for us to, uh, visit, Addy," John said quickly, edging toward the door.

"Sorry." Addy yawned and stretched, sensuously she hoped. "I thought we'd have the house to ourselves longer. Maybe next time."

"There won't be a next time, Christain. Get out."

"Right. Whatever you say. Addy, about... ?"

"Everything will be fine," Addy said. The relief on John's face told her he understood the reference to his car. He'd played his part; she'd leave his car alone.

As the door closed behind him, Addy rose lithely from the sofa and moved over to sit at the table. She felt more secure with a solid piece of furniture between her and Sam.

"Perhaps I'd be more entertained by your performance if I understood the point of it. Would you button that damned shirt! If you were trying to make me jealous, forget it."

"I wasn't." Addy rolled clay between her palms. If she bedded the entire staff at John's hotel she couldn't make Sam jealous. He didn't care enough for jealousy.

"Well?"

She tightened her fist around the lump of clay so tightly the clay oozed between her fingers. "I did not give you the right to interrogate me."

"You don't think our scheduled wedding tomorrow gives me the right to ask a few questions about why you invited Christain up to your bedroom?"

"We weren't in my bedroom."

"I suppose you weren't making love on the sofa, either."

"No, we weren't." Addy paused to study the clay log she'd rolled. "Not yet."

"Not yet," he repeated softly. "You intended to make love to another man the day before our wedding?"

"It's not the day before my wedding. I told you I wasn't going to marry you. You chose to ignore that." She mashed up the amateurishly misshapen log and tried again. "I've been free and single for a long time. I don't want to tie myself down to one man. I prefer my social life to be like this room, cluttered and chaotic. Even if I thought I could stand being monogamous, it wouldn't work with you. Not with all that traveling you do. I'd be too lonely. And tempted."

Addy's hands shook and nerves roiled her stomach. She prayed her next words convinced Sam. "I admit, marriage to you would solve a number of my problems, and I considered it, but although you might not think so, I do occasionally have a conscience. You were kind enough to offer to marry me. The least I can do is refuse. You aren't the kind of man who'd like sharing his wife." Her heart pounded so fiercely, blood hammered against her eardrums.

An eternity passed before Sam spoke. "I'll explain to Grandmother and the others for you."

"Thank you. Hannah said you were leaving Sunday morning. I'll have the necklace finished before you leave."

"You don't need to—"

"I don't take charity," Addy snapped, looking squarely at Sam for the first time since he'd walked through her doorway. Her stomach recoiled at the fury blazing from his blue eyes. The jaw she'd labeled pugnacious had solidified into rock-hard granite. She fought a craven urge to flee as Sam stalked across the room. He didn't stop until the only thing between them was the table which seemed suddenly flimsy.

"You'll take this." Sam tossed a package gift-wrapped in white onto the hard plastic sheet she worked on. "You don't have to call it a wedding present." He practically sneered the words. "Like you, I pay my debts." Turning on his heel, he strode from the room.

Addy picked up the package with trembling fingers. She didn't want to open it. The ribbon fell to the table. She didn't want a present from Sam Dawson. The paper crinkled loudly as she cast it aside. Addy eyed the white jeweler's box with trepidation, until she gathered the courage to remove the lid and lift aside the blanket of white cotton. Her throat swelled with painful tears as she looked at the contents of the box. She squeezed the cardboard box so tightly it split with a loud snap. Resting on a bed of cotton was a coil of silver chain encircling a small silver charm. A replica of an old-fashioned clothespin.

CHAPTER NINE

ADDY brushed a nonexistent piece of lint from her lap as she steered her car north on Interstate 25 toward Denver early Saturday morning. Brushed it away as easily as she'd brushed Sam Dawson from her life. Sam had obviously talked to his grandmother as promised. When Addy told Hannah last night she and Emilie would be moving out the first of the week, Hannah had made no comments, asked no questions. Not wanting to see the hurt and disgust on the older woman's face, Addy had concentrated on peeling carrots for the casserole she'd cooked Sam and his grandmother for dinner. Emilie had spent the night at her friend's house, and Addy had dined in solitary splendor on a cheeseburger at a fast-food restaurant.

This morning a quick phone call to the mother of Emilie's friend had arranged for Emilie to stay there until Addy came for her. The woman had readily agreed, thinking Addy had last-minute wedding details to attend to. Addy hadn't bothered to set her straight. By noon everyone up and down Ute Pass would know the wedding had been called off. She shouldn't feel guilty leaving the task to four elderly ladies. They'd arranged the wedding without the bride's help. They could un-arrange it the same way.

A loud bang jolted Addy from her thoughts. The car swerved wildly, and Addy jerked her foot from the gas pedal, fighting to bring the car under control, at the same time guiding it to the side of the busy highway. Thankfully she'd been in the right-hand lane. The car coasted slower and slower until Addy could safely, gently apply the brakes. The vehicle bumped and bucked to a halt.

Addy collapsed against the back of the seat, waiting for her racing heart to settle down before she stepped from the car. She was in no hurry to view the damage. In the rearview mirror she saw a few shreds of what had been her tire blow off the highway in the wake of a speeding semi-truck.

Putting off the inevitable didn't make it go away. Addy slid over to get out of the car through the passenger side door. The car rested drunkenly slanted to one side, the right front wheel resting on its rim.

She hadn't dressed this morning to change a tire, but life wasn't giving her a lot of options. Tossing into the car the pale gray jacket of the suit she'd purchased yesterday from a thrift shop, Addy opened the car trunk and extracted the jack and tire iron. She hoisted her skirt above her knees and squatted in the dirt beside the car. A short time later fat bolts dotted the ground, and the shredded tire rested against the opened car trunk. She reached for the spare. It was flat as a pancake.

Addy wanted to scream. On her way to the most important meeting of her life, she was stranded halfway between Colorado Springs and Castle Rock, miles from the nearest gas station. She had filthy hands, and three large black oily streaks marred the front of her skirt. She'd broken two fingernails and ripped her blouse when she'd lost her balance and tumbled backward into the dirt. She didn't want to know what the back of her skirt looked like.

"Darn." Addy kicked the nearest tire, understanding completely how people got so angry with their cars they shot them. Her foot smarted, and she looked down to see half the polish scuffed off the toe of her shoe. "Darn and double darn." She kicked the car again. Pain shot up her leg, and she leaned on the side of the car, beating against the roof with her fists. At first the sound of spitting gravel signaling a car pulling off the highway onto the road shoulder behind her didn't register. The half-amused, half-exasperated voice got her immediate attention.

"Got a problem, Adeline?"

She wouldn't look up. She would not look up. She looked up. Sam leaned out his opened window. Addy slowly straightened. She wanted to deny she had a problem. She wanted to tell him to go away. Too much was at stake to do so. "What are you doing here?"

"I'm on my way to Denver." Checking for a break in traffic, he stepped from the car. "Blowout?"

"No, I'm having a little picnic breakfast beside the road."

"Good thing I found out before I married you how surly you are in the morning." His eyebrows lifted as he took in her appearance. "You going to a costume party?"

Addy swallowed an angry sob. "I'm meeting someone, a man." She emphasized the last word. "For breakfast."

"Odd choice of clothes for a rendezvous."

His eyes seemed to pierce the white blouse she wore. Addy forced herself to keep her hands from flying up to hide the silver charm hanging on its chain beneath the blouse. Sam couldn't possibly see it. "Just because you prefer white lab coats."

Sam laughed. "I've yet to meet the man who has fantasies about kissing a woman who's dressed like a stereotype of a suburban housewife on her way to a parent-teacher's meeting."

Addy stiffened. His gibing remark came perilously close to the truth. "I didn't realize men discussed their fantasies with each other."

"There's a lot you don't realize, but we'll discuss that later. Hop in. I'll give you a ride."

"Only to the nearest filling station."

"Let me open the trunk." A minute later he said, "Damn it, Adeline, I intended to get that." He took the spare tire from her and slung it into Hannah's car trunk. "Need anything from your car?"

"No. I'll be back as soon as the filling station fixes the flat tire."

"I don't think so." Sam stood at the front of her car looking down at the wheel. "The rim's bent. They'll have to send a tow truck. You can't drive this car anywhere."

"I have to," Addy wailed. "I can't miss my appointment."

"I could drive you," Sam offered.

Not if she had anything to say about it.

Why she ever dreamed she might, she couldn't imagine. She hadn't had anything to say about anything from the moment Sam Dawson walked into his grandmother's house. He was an overbearing, interfering bully. Even his grandmother called him bossy. "I never knew a man so intent on having his own way as you are."

"You're grumpy when you skip breakfast, aren't you?"

"I'm not grumpy. My car let me down, and repairs will probably cost me a small fortune." How was she going to pay them? With jewelry? Without her car, how could she get away with Emilie? Addy crossed her fingers in her lap, praying for the success of her upcoming meeting. If the man had waited, if she could successfully convince him to direct his search back East, she'd have more time. Surreptitiously she checked her watch for the tenth time in as many minutes. "I'm late," she said, again for the tenth time in as many minutes.

The clothes covering her body didn't bear thinking about. Between the grease and grime, not to mention rips, she'd been forced to change out of her suit. Her selections had been extremely limited. Limited to two items, in fact. A garish yellow that defied description colored the sweatshirt Belle had left on the backseat of Hannah's car which Sam drove. Addy had purchased the lime green sweatpants at the thrift shop to cut into a play outfit for Emilie. She'd forgotten to take them out of her car yesterday. Her old electric teal blue caftan faded in comparison to this outfit.

Sam pulled up in front of the huge hotel doors. "You're meeting him here?"

"It's a hotel. Where else would I meet a man?"

"I meant, why so far west? Why not downtown or near the Tech Center on the south side of Denver?"

"He's coming from Vail." He was coming from the airport. She'd told him she was driving in from Vail. Addy jumped from the car. "Thanks. You needn't wait. He'll take me back." There must be buses. She slammed the door and ran into the hotel before Sam could respond.

Addy stopped first in the hotel ladies' room. Minutes later, she resigned herself to the fact that little more could be done to improve her appearance. Strands of hair straggled from the tight bun, and washing the dirt from her face had removed most of her makeup. She'd driven down Ute Pass three hours earlier the picture, or so she'd hoped, of a young society matron. The proper mother of a young girl. Now she looked like a rodeo clown in training who'd already tangled with the bull. And lost.

Looking at her watch again, her heart sank at the advanced hour. Please, let him have waited. She had to put him off, gain more time, misdirect him.

Giving her bedraggled image one last despairing scowl, Addy took a deep breath and went to find the man who would claim to be Emilie's father.

He sat in the hotel coffee shop, his gaze locked on the entrance. If he hadn't been wearing the red carnation in his buttonhole, Addy would have walked right past him. This white-haired, somewhat portly, seventy-something man was Lorie's mysterious, passionate lover? Her gaze swept the coffee shop. No other man wore a red flower.

Explaining to the hostess she was meeting someone, Addy pinned a confident smile on her face and walked over to the table. "I'm sorry I'm late. I had a tire blowout," she said.

The man looked at her, did a double take at her clothing, then slowly pushed back his chair and stood up. Reaching for her hand, he clung to it, his eyes searching her face. After a moment, he gave a little shake to his head, and gave her a tentative smile. "Thank you for seeing me. I hoped you'd bring the child, but I suppose that was too much to ask."

"I'm Addy Johnson. Lorie's sister and Emilie's aunt and guardian. I'm afraid my husband couldn't come today. Business. Not that he's one of those men who pays more attention to business than to his family. Emilie always comes first with him, I assure you." She'd rehearsed her speech a thousand times.

"Emilie," the man said. "A nice old-fashioned name. Does the little girl look like her mother? Her mother was astonishingly beautiful. But you know that, I'm sorry, I'm rattling to no purpose. It's just, I was surprised, you know, when you called Thursday. When I received no answer to my first two letters, I was afraid . . . I'm sorry, as you've guessed, I'm William Burgess." He dipped his head in an old-fashioned gesture. "Please. I apologize. I'm keeping you standing, and you had a blowout, and I haven't even asked if you're all right. Please sit down." He hesitated. "I'd like to meet the child."

Addy sat, clenching her hands in her lap. "I'd like some coffee and something to eat."

"Of course. Excuse me. You must think I'm terribly rude." He beckoned a waiter to take Addy's order. "About Emilie—"

"Why do you want to see her now? The papers giving me custody are all in order." She hoped they were.

William Burgess straightened up at the hostility in her voice. He seemed to be considering how to answer.

"Adeline. Honey, there you— What the hell happened to you? Where's your car? I didn't see it in the parking lot."

Addy's mouth gaped open. Lack of breakfast must be making her hallucinate. She shook her head to clear it. Sam stood beside her chair. "A blowout," she managed to say. She should have known Sam Dawson wouldn't do as he'd been told.

"Damn it, Adeline, I told you that damned clunker wouldn't make it to Denver. You OK?" Bending down, he pressed a hard, possessive kiss on her mouth. "Wives," he said with husbandly resignation, pulling out a chair and joining them at the table. "I told her to rent a car." He looked across the table. "I'm Adeline's husband, Sam Dawson. You must be Burgess."

Clearly taken aback at the antagonism on Sam's face, William Burgess didn't make the mistake of offering to shake hands. "Please. Call me Bill." The look on Sam's face made it clear whatever Sam would like to call Burgess, it wasn't Bill. Hastily turning to Addy, Burgess said, "When you told me your name, Addy, I assumed you'd married a man also named Johnson, but I guess you kept your maiden name."

"Ms. Johnson to you," Sam snarled.

"Yes, of course." Almost shyly, Burgess scrutinized Addy's face. "You don't look much like Loraine."

"I take after my father's side of the family."

"Are your parents, Emilie's grandparents, living?"

"Cut the social chitchat, Burgess, and let's get down to business. I've consulted my wife's and my attorney." In an aside to Addy, Sam said, "I gave Jim Carlson a retainer."

The room started spinning around Addy. She grabbed Sam's hand to keep from falling off her chair. "A retainer," she echoed weakly. "For what?"

Sam ignored her, his attention riveted on William Burgess. "Our attorney is prepared to file an injunction against you and get a court order to keep you from harassing Addy. She's Emilie's aunt and guardian, and for all intents and purposes, Emilie's mother, and always has been, and it's a little late for you to even think about any kind of custody. I had our lawyer check, and Loraine Johnson's lawyer has a copy of the paper you and Loraine signed."

"Paper?" William Burgess looked blankly at Sam. "I didn't sign any paper."

"Tell it to the judge," Sam sneered. "You had the damned thing notarized."

"There's some mistake," Burgess said.

"Right," Sam said tersely. "You made it. If you thought you could bully Adeline, forget it. Not only will you have to go through the courts to get to her, you'll have to go through me, since I'm her husband, and through the rest of her family. We're all prepared to testify to what a wonderful mother Addy is."

Burgess looked as stunned as Addy felt. "I'm sure Addy—Ms. Johnson is a wonderful mother." He wiped his face with his napkin. "I never intended..." His words trailed off as the waiter brought Addy her scrambled eggs.

Sam took one look at Addy's pale face and ordered, "Eat. And don't give me any lip about not being hungry. You're shaking." He called the waiter back. "Bring her some decaffeinated coffee. And bring me a cup of regular." Sam gave Addy a fierce look. "I told you to eat."

She didn't know whether to laugh or bawl. She said, "I'm right-handed."

"Damn it, Adeline, I don't give a damn... Oh." Sam released the hand he held in a steel grip. "Sorry."

While the waiter went after their coffee, Addy doggedly ate her eggs. If she didn't, Sam Dawson would probably spoon-feed her.

Sam Dawson lied for her. The words kept repeating in her brain. Sam Dawson lied for her. Yesterday he'd seen her rolling on the sofa with John Christain, and today he was in Denver standing—sitting—at her side. Lying for her.

She choked down another bite of eggs. It was one thing for Addy Johnson to arrange to meet William Burgess with every intention of looking him right in the eye and swearing to a bunch of big fat lies. Such as she was married. Married and vacationing in Vail, Colorado, at her husband's relatives' house. Married and residing in Boston, Massachusetts, where her husband based his business. She hadn't planned to use Sam's name.

Unless she had to. The eggs seemed to multiply on her plate. The more she ate, the more yellow lumps covered the heavy white china. She hated cold toast, orange marmalade, burnt bacon and greasy hashed brown potatoes. The look on Sam's face told her he expected her to eat every bite.

He'd lied for her.

She'd tried to convince him she and John Christain were well on their way to being lovers, and he'd lied for her. She'd been going to use him, and he'd lied for her. How he knew what she was doing, where she was going, whom she planned to meet barely concerned Addy at this point.

He'd lied for her.

She wondered if his grandmother knew. Addy's throat tightened, rejecting the eggs. "Hannah?" she croaked.

"Emilie was tired and didn't want to stay at her friend's house. Grandmother thought it best if she stayed at home with Squirt." Sam looked squarely at Burgess. "My grandmother has lived in Colorado a long time and knows everyone worth knowing. She's wealthy, and we have two doctors in the family. I'm telling you so you'll know there's money and power behind Adeline. Pick a fight with her, and you'll have to take us all on, and believe me, Burgess, the Dawsons fight to win. No court in the land would take Emilie away from my wife, but if you don't quit hassling Adeline, we'll make you pay."

Addy grabbed the charm hanging from her neck. A lifesaver in this turbulent sea of insanity. Sam Dawson, a man of logic and science, who constantly preached calm and reason, had not only lied, now he was issuing threats. Next he'd be brawling in the middle of the hotel coffee shop. Addy couldn't allow this to continue. Shaking her head, she smiled mistily at Sam. "Thank you, but you mustn't..." She had to stop to wipe her leaking eyes with her napkin. "It's all a lie, Mr. Burgess. Sam and I aren't married. He's a friend." She pressed her fist against her mouth for a minute as she fought for control. "A very good friend, but not my husband. And we don't have a lawyer. I can't afford a lawyer.

"The truth is, Mr. Burgess, I live barely a step above needing foodstamps. I know you can give Emilie expensive toys and clothes, any material thing she wants, but what I can't give her in money, I give her in love." She pressed the silver clothespin painfully against her skin.

"I came to tell you I was married and lived back east. While you were searching for us there, I intended to pack up Emilie and run, changing our names and going into hiding."

Addy clutched the hand Sam held out to her, and looked across the table. "But I can't let Sam lie for me." She raised her chin. "I can't let you have Emilie, either. I don't know how I'll do it, but I'll fight you with every breath left in my body. I can't, I won't let you destroy Emilie the way you destroyed my sister."

"But I never met your sister."

Dead silence greeted Burgess's announcement. In the background a piece of silverware fell to the floor with a loud clang. Shock paralyzed every muscle in Addy's body.

Sam finally stirred. "Who the hell are you if you're not Emilie's father?"

"I think, I hope, I'm her grandfather."

Addy squeezed Sam's hand with both of hers. Not Emilie's father.

Sam leaned forward, his eyes, dangerously dark, pinned on the elderly man. "Why the threatening letters to Addy?"

"I never intended them to be threatening. I wanted to pique the interest of the child's parents."

"Why the secret about who you are?" Sam demanded to know.

Burgess gave Addy an apologetic smile. "I should have told you in the beginning, but... I don't know what you know of your sister's life in California." He broke off, distress and a reluctance to continue written all over his face.

"I know she fell in with bad company and committed suicide," Addy said quietly. "I know your son—I assume your son?" At Burgess's nod, she continued. "I know he's married."

Burgess shook his head. "He got drunk and wrapped his car around a tree trunk a few months ago. The police assured me he died instantly."

After a moment Addy reached across the table and rested her hand on his. "I'm sorry. I know how difficult it is to accept sudden death. Not to have a chance to say goodbye."

"We hadn't talked for a long time. I worked hard over the years and my business prospered, but my family suffered. Foolishly, I thought if I made more money, I could make things right. I was wrong. My wife was an alcoholic. One night when I didn't come home for dinner as I'd promised, she fell down the stairs and broke her neck. Willie was twenty years old. He never forgave me.'' Burgess took a swallow of coffee.

"Willie's wife told me about your sister after Willie died. Marilyn was bitter. Willie didn't leave her with much. I paid her a large sum of money for Willie's effects. I thought, now it's too late, I might get to know him. Pathetic, isn't it?" Burgess gave a ironic laugh when no one disagreed with him.

"I found some letters from your sister and discovered there had been a child, so I hired a private detective. I married late in life, and I'm seventy years old. I failed my wife and my son. I hoped I'd get another chance. With Emilie. Not to take her away from you, Ms. Johnson. To get to know her. If you don't want her to claim me as her grandfather, I'd understand, but I beg you to let me at least meet her.''

"I still don't understand why you didn't tell Addy who you are," Sam said.

Burgess gave Addy a shame-faced smile. "Willie gave Lorraine large sums of money for the child. From what my detective found out, Loraine spent it all on herself. I couldn't be sure Ms. Johnson wasn't the same. I want to contribute financially to Emilie's upbringing, but I didn't want to be held for ransom, especially if Emilie wasn't my son's child.''

Addy stiffened. "I didn't agree to meet you to inveigle money from you. Just because I said we were hard up doesn't mean I want your money, your charity or your pity.''

"It's not charity to set up a trust fund for my only granddaughter. Teenagers are expensive. There are things like braces and sports and music or dancing lessons. College costs have sky-rocketed.''

"Don't worry about Emilie," Sam said evenly, "her family will take care of her. You heard Addy. She doesn't like charity.''

Addy wasn't sure if Sam meant his remark as an insult, so she ignored it. Her hand still rested on William Burgess's hand. She gave him a pat and leaned back in her chair. "I think, Mr. Burgess—" she smiled hesitantly "—Bill, the best thing is for you to come to Colorado Springs and meet Emilie. As for telling Emilie who you are and any future trust funds, why don't we sort of let nature take its course?"

"I thought you said you were coming from Vail."

Addy colored. "Another lie to put you off our track. We live in a small town west of Colorado Springs, up Ute Pass."

"I understand. I shouldn't have said anything. It's just..." He took out a white handkerchief and blew his nose, "when I heard about your sister, I thought she was a cheap little home-wrecker. After meeting you... I suppose my son... He was spoiled. I gave him money instead of time, and my wife, well, she wanted him on her side. If you hated all Burgesses, I wouldn't blame you. You're a kind, generous, good person, Ms. Johnson."

Addy shook her head. "No, I'm a very selfish person, a coward and much too proud. Sam offered me money to hire someone to find out who was behind the letters, but I was too proud to take his help. I told myself what I was doing was best for Emilie, but the truth is, what I cared about is losing her. Instead of fighting for her, I was prepared to run away, to lie. Even worse, to teach her to lie. I'm not a good person, and I don't deserve to have a friend like Sam." She sent a wobbly smile in his direction. "I know you came for Emilie's sake, Sam, and I appreciate it. Thank you."

"Adeline!" Sam said explosively. He stopped and grabbed his cup of coffee and drank deeply.

She eyed him in bewilderment. "What?"

"Shut up and eat your damned breakfast."

* * *

They rode in silence for almost an hour. The towering landmark rock above the town of Castle Rock loomed over them before Addy worked up enough courage to ask the question which had gnawed at her since they left the hotel. "How did you know what I was doing this morning and where I was going?"

Sam stared straight ahead, his jaw carved from stone. "Snooped. When you rushed out so early dressed like a PTA reject, I thought you were running away. Grandmother knew where Emilie'd spent the night, so I tore over there, to find you'd made arrangements for them to keep Emilie until midday. I knew you'd never leave without Emilie."

"But you took Emilie home to Hannah just in case," Addy said slowly.

"When I started to leave her friend's house, Emilie fussed and fretted so I took her with me, and Grandmother thought it best if they stayed behind while I came to Denver."

"How did you know where I'd gone?"

"The letters. I knew where you kept them."

"You went through my drawers?" she asked, outraged.

"Yes, Adeline, I went through your drawers. I was desperate. Rereading the last letter convinced me you'd arranged to meet the man. He'd listed two phone numbers on the letter, his home phone and his work phone. I called both and eventually reached his secretary. I convinced her it was crucial I locate him, and she told me where he was staying." He gave Addy a dry look. "You're not the only one who knows how to lie."

"At least I don't brag about it."

Sam snorted. "I didn't know if you were meeting him there, but I had no other lead. It was just luck you broke down on the road and I found you so I could get to the hotel the same time you did."

"I'd hardly call it luck to have a blowout on the interstate."

"I don't think we want to discuss the missing brain cells which prompted you to drive that broken-down heap to Denver," Sam said coldly. He went on. "I parked in front of the hotel and when you didn't come out, I figured you were meeting him there. I checked the coffee shop first. You know the rest."

"I don't know," Addy said carefully, fiddling with the charm hanging from her neck, "why you came to Denver. I don't know why you told Bill you and I are married. I don't know what I'm going to do about my car. I don't know how I'm going to explain to Emilie about her grandfather."

"What an awful lot of stuff you don't know," Sam said.

The amusement in his voice failed to endear him to her. He was supposed to fall on his knees, figuratively speaking of course since he was driving, and tell her he loved her. He'd said he was good at lying. Couldn't he tell the one lie she longed to hear?

CHAPTER TEN

"WE SHOULD have brought Bill back with us," Addy said into the silence.

Sam shook his head. "He'd have pestered you about Emilie all the way back. Besides, he's better off renting a car so he'll have his own transportation once he gets here."

"I don't think Hannah would have minded if he stayed at the house."

"I would have," Sam said firmly. "He'll be fine at the hotel. He may be Emilie's grandfather, but he doesn't need to be underfoot. All you know about him is what he told us. Let's take this slow. It won't hurt him to serve a kind of probation before you welcome him into the family with open arms. Just because he told you a heart-rending story about failing his family and wanting a second chance, doesn't make it true. Let Emilie set the pace."

"Emilie," Addy scoffed. "She'd welcome Dracula with open arms. She likes everyone."

"She didn't like Christain." Sam shot Addy a quick glance.

"I don't care to discuss John with you." Addy hated the defensive tone in her voice. "You may have pretended to be my husband this morning, but my private life is my own business."

"Your private life is my business when you're engaged to me," Sam snapped. "How do you think I felt when I walked in and saw Christain pawing you?"

"Relieved, I would imagine."

"Relieved!" Sam said explosively. "I couldn't decide whose neck I wanted to wring first. His or yours."

"Oh, please. You only asked me to marry you because you felt sorry for me, and you stated outright that nothing I did could make you jealous, not that I was interested in making you jealous. How dog-in-the-mangerish of you to get annoyed when you thought John might be interested in me. You know you're happy to get rid of me."

"Happy," Sam repeated in a contemplative voice. "First I was relieved, now I'm happy." He headed the car across the opposite lane of Highway 24 and onto the side road to town. "Is Christain interested in you?"

"None of your business."

"Are you interested in him?"

Addy stuck her nose in the air.

"Don't you want to know what Emilie said about him?"

Not in a million years.

"I asked her, if I'm a chocolate cupcake, and Addy's a kangaroo, what is Christain? She thought about six seconds before she asked what you call the stuff you use a knife on to get it out of Grandmother's old freezer when you melt it. Her description." When Addy didn't respond, Sam said, "Sounds like she meant frost." A minute later he casually added, "I guess that freezes Christain out of the picture." He smirked at his own joke. "We both know you aren't about to embark on any relationship Emilie disapproves of."

"The only man I know whom Emilie approves of is you," Addy said without thinking.

"Emilie is a very bright little girl."

Since wholesale mayhem wasn't an option for civilized people, Addy refrained from commenting on either Sam's remark or the smug expression on his face.

Sam drove past two unfamiliar cars parked in front of Hannah's house and pulled the car into the driveway.

Instead of opening his door, he stopped Addy as she reached for her door handle. He stared intently across the yard. "I'll be damned," he said softly. "Stay here." He stepped from the car.

Something about his tone of voice cemented Addy in her seat. Rolling down her window, she looked in the direction Sam headed, but saw nothing except the neighbor's small poodle playing with a short stick. Squatting down, Sam called the dog. Stick in mouth, the dog galloped to Sam's side. A short, friendly tussle ensued, Sam laughing and the dog barking. Then Sam stood up and walked toward the car, the stick in his hand. The dog bounced and yelped at his side until Sam picked up another stick and hurled it toward the dog's yard. The dog raced after the stick.

Sam gave Addy a crooked smile. "A little the worse for wear, but at least recognizable."

Addy took a second look. She hadn't recognized it. "My great-grandmother's clothespin."

Sam drew back when she reached for it. "It's filthy. I think we better give it a little session in the oven to toast any microorganisms which have taken up residence."

"I can't believe you found it."

"Maybe it means this is my lucky day." He opened the car door. "My guess is Emilie is sound asleep, but I know you'll want to go straight up and check on her."

Sam was right. Emilie slept soundly, a ragged Sam the Bear hugged close to her small, warm body. Addy shut the bedroom door and walked across the sitting room to the front window, brushing aside the lace curtain. The two cars remained in front of the house. One of the neighbors must have company. Parking space on the hillside was scarce, and everyone understood cars straggled along the street. It was a good neighborhood with good people.

She'd miss them. The sun slipped behind a cloud. Shadows turned gray the pale pink wild roses climbing the wall and stole the color from the delicate-looking poppies along the front walk. A small dark shape flashed shrilly past the window and dove to attack. A rufous hummingbird chasing away a broad-tailed hummingbird. Two black and white magpies squabbled rancorously in the large blue spruce.

Weariness sapped the strength from Addy's bones. What now? If Bill Burgess had told the truth, she no longer had to worry about Emilie being torn from her. If only she'd answered his first letter instead of letting fear rule her decisions. If only she'd swallowed her pride and borrowed money to hire a lawyer. If only she hadn't fallen in love with Sam and acted the complete fool. If only... Her "if only's" could fill a book.

She turned her back to the window. The sun broke from under the clouds and glared harshly into the sitting room picking out the tarnish on silver frames and the bedraggled edges of the silk flowers on an old hat. The strong light treated unkindly her mother's amateurish paintings and spotlighted the worn areas on the furniture. The room no longer looked warm and inviting. It looked gaudy and shabby and cheap. Draped and decorated like a vaudeville theater set, the room didn't belong in an old Victorian house which was rich with understated elegance and the patina of a long and happy family life.

Addy didn't belong here, either. Hannah wouldn't tell her she had to move, but Addy wasn't so blind she couldn't see how awkward it would be to stay. Hannah had seen her not once, not twice, but three times involved in compromising situations. As much as Addy wished it were otherwise, she could blame no one but herself for totally messing up.

Sam rapped twice at the closed sitting room door and breezed into the room carrying a napkin-covered plate.

"Knock, knock. Come in, Sam. Thank you." He held the plate out to Addy. "A late lunch. It's almost three o'clock, and you barely touched your breakfast. Eat. And take your hair out of that stupid thing."

Not bothering to explain again the protocol about knocking on doors, Addy set the plate on the table. "Thank you." If she tried to eat, her churning stomach would revolt.

Sam strolled over to the sofa and stretched out, his arms folded behind his head. "You shouldn't have to worry anymore about losing custody of Emilie."

"I hope not." She wished he'd leave.

"And I guess you don't think it's necessary anymore to marry for Emilie's sake."

"No."

"So if you were to get married, say later this afternoon, you wouldn't be doing it for Emilie, you'd be doing it because you wanted to."

"I'm not getting married this afternoon."

"Hypothetical question."

"Hypothetically," Addy said carefully, "if I were getting married, I'd do it because I wanted to."

"Do you want to?"

Sam asked the question so casually, it took a second before his words sunk in. "Do I want to what?" Addy asked, thinking she'd misunderstood the question.

"Get married this afternoon. You know, wear the old wedding dress, carry the pink roses, meet my family, eat cake, drink champagne. All that stuff that happens at weddings."

The meaning behind his cavalier words slowly percolated through to Addy's brain. "You didn't stop them," she said, stunned. "You didn't call off the wedding."

"Did you ever try to stop an avalanche with a snow shovel?"

Chilled, Addy rubbed her arms in a futile effort to get warm. "You expect me to marry you simply because you couldn't figure out how to call off the wedding?" An image of the two unfamiliar cars parked out front popped into her mind. "Your family's here? For the wedding?" She shivered. She must be coming down with the flu.

"Sometimes life's easier if you just go with the flow."

Sam sounded sincere. To hear him talk, he'd rather marry Addy than fight his grandmother. The man who'd been successfully defeating his mother's and grandmother's matchmaking schemes since he'd turned thirty? Nothing about this scenario made sense. After all that had happened, he couldn't possibly be expecting Addy to go through with the wedding.

It was a bad dream. She squeezed her eyes tightly shut, counted to ten, and opened them. Sam watched her from his recumbent position on the sofa. "Why didn't you stop them?" she asked. "Why are you allowing them to railroad you into this? You don't want to marry me. You can't deny all the times you've said so."

"I meant it every time I said it. Don't interrupt. And let your damned hair down. I hate it that way."

It said something for the state of Addy's mind that, without a word, she obediently removed the pins from her hair, allowing it to fall to her shoulders.

Sam nodded his approval before continuing. "I had my life charted out, and marriage wasn't on the agenda for a few years. I told you why, my traveling and so on. When the time did come, I knew exactly the kind of wife I'd select."

"Not my kind. You said so often enough."

"And in saying so, I violated a basic tenet of science. I reached a conclusion before I had enough data to support that conclusion."

"I'm not talking about a cure for bad breath. I'm talking about marriage. About my life." Before she succumbed to hysteria, Addy wanted to know one thing. "Are you asking me because you want to marry *me,* Adeline Johnson, or because the ladies booked the church and ordered oysters?"

"What's with the damned oysters? Belle wanted to know if I liked oysters. When I said no, she said she doubted I'd need them anyway."

"Never mind the oysters. You don't have to marry me. I gave you an out."

"John Christain," Sam said. "You set up that whole scene for my benefit. You wanted me to catch you. So I'd have an excuse for calling off the wedding. You thought I didn't want to marry you."

"You don't." Addy took a deep breath. "Do you?"

"I admit, Adeline, I don't understand it myself, but the odd truth is, yes, I do want to marry you."

Addy sank into the nearest chair. "Are you saying," she asked, determined Sam spell out his feelings, "you love me?"

"Adeline, I have advanced degrees in chemistry and business management. I excel at logic and reasoning. It's neither logical nor reasonable for a man to meet a woman and in the space of three weeks fall madly in love with her."

"I see." She didn't. Not yet. She would before she gave him her answer. Or maybe she'd just strangle him. "You viewed the situation calmly and objectively and decided you wanted to marry me." Saying the words out loud didn't improve them or make them easier to comprehend. She wouldn't strangle him. She'd smother him in an enormous jar of peanut butter. "I suppose you have data to support this particular, peculiar conclusion."

"I've given it some thought."

"Some thought." She'd add grape jelly to the jar. Lots of grape jelly. "Would you care to share your thought?" She silently applauded how well she was behaving in the face of extraordinary provocation. She hoped the judge at her murder trial took her phenomenal restraint into consideration.

Sam rearranged the pillows behind his back. "You said you wanted to marry a man who likes purple, is rich, drives a red sport car, has a large house, is dependable and comes with a large family who'll love and cherish Emilie. I'm not rich, but I can afford for you to shop wherever you want. Granted I drive a black sedan, but I can trade it in, although I have to tell you, Adeline, a sedan is more practical for a large family. Pick out a big house and I'll buy it for you. My bank, my employees, my clients, my family—they'll all tell you I'm dependable."

He wasn't telling her what she wanted to hear. She opened her mouth, but Sam hadn't finished.

"Grandmother already adores Emilie. Emilie captivated the rest of them the minute they walked in the door from the airport. Mom says she can already tell her first granddaughter is going to follow in her footsteps and be a great actress."

Addy's ribcage shrank until every breath brought pain. "You hate purple."

"You see, there's that insufficient data thing raising its ugly head again. I always thought I hated purple. Three weeks ago if anyone asked me if I'd like a purple room, I wouldn't have hesitated to give them a resounding no."

"Three weeks ago?" He'd met her three weeks ago.

"Well, maybe two and a half. That was when I started fantasizing about a purple bedroom, a red and green striped bed with big, fat soft pillows in every shade of the rainbow, and you sprawled in the middle waiting for me."

"In a white lab coat."

"Hell, no." A wry grin slanted his mouth. "I made up the white lab coat to tease you." His grin disappeared. "In my fantasy you wore bright blue gauzy stuff. And had bare feet."

The blue eyes blazing across the room at her sent a message. Addy ignored the tingling in her breasts. Being wanted was nice, but she was greedy. She wanted much more. "That's why you want to marry me? Because I made up a shopping list of the attributes I wanted my future husband to have, and you think you have them?"

"Partly. And partly it's because I want secret messages on my walls and I want my kids to have a mother like you." Sam hesitated before adding fiercely, "And I want you to smile at me the way you smile at Emilie. All warm and accepting and soft and marshmallowy. In fact," he said slowly with deep satisfaction, "exactly how you're smiling at me now."

Addy hurtled across the room and flung herself full-length on Sam's half-reclining body. "I love you, Dr. Samuel Dawson, Ph.D. I want you to know I decided I did after viewing the situation calmly and objectively." There was nothing calm or objective about the kiss she gave him.

His hands cupped warmly around her bottom. "You've never viewed a situation calmly and objectively in your life."

"Yes, I have. I knew at once you were a purple bedroom kind of guy." She nibbled on his ear. She loved his ears. "I structured the deal to meet your particular wants and needs."

"I'm not adverse to a discussion of my wants and needs," he said, punctuating his words with kisses, "and your selling points. Not to mention packaging. That yellow thing has got to go."

Addy giggled. She'd forgotten she wore Belle's sweatshirt. "You're the expert. What kind of packaging did you have in mind?"

"Freckles. Nothing but freckles."

Sam's mouth swallowed the rest of Addy's giggles, and soon other, more intense desires swamped any desire to giggle.

"Sam?" Addy stirred on the sofa beneath Sam, the offensive yellow sweatshirt long ago cast aside.

Sam lifted his head from Addy's chest. "What?"

"Do you really think we'll work out? We're so different and I've never lived in Boston, and—"

"Do you want to? I've been thinking—"

"When you weren't fantasizing," she teased, running her hand over the top of his head. She loved the rasp of his short hair against her palm.

"When I wasn't fantasizing," he muttered into her open, laughing mouth. Minutes later, he raised his head. "I can have my office anywhere. Why not here? It wouldn't take much arranging, and when I'm out of town, you'll have lots of support. Grandmother is talking about moving to an apartment. She says this house is too much for her. Why don't we buy it?" His eyes darkened. "Lots of bedrooms you could fill with kids."

"I suppose you'd want to consult on that project."

"Definitely." He smiled down at her. "As a scientist, I've never believed in witches, but I'm beginning to think you're one. I don't know what else explains why, from the moment I walked into this house and met you, I wanted to be in this room. I'd lay awake nights inventing excuses to come in here. You cast a spell on me."

Addy gave him a guileless smile. "Not me. My mother's paintings. When you look at them, all you see are globs of color, but actually they're subliminal messages telling you freckles are better than chocolate." Her voice barely quivered with amusement.

Sam nipped at her bottom lip. "I planned to talk you into hanging those paintings in Emilie's room, but maybe we better put them in our bedroom."

"You mean you wouldn't prefer chocolate?"

"That reminds me. Belle suggested chocolate for the honeymoon. I have no idea what she was talking about. Does it occur to you those women are fixated on food? Do you suppose they're anorexic or something?"

The look on his face when Addy dissolved into gales of laughter made her laugh all the harder.

Sam stared down at her, bright flames dancing in the back of his eyes. "The brilliant Dr. Dawson does not appreciate being laughed at. If you don't discontinue your inappropriate behavior, the brilliant Dr. Dawson will be forced to conduct an experiment to discover if kissing can stop laughter."

Several minutes later, Addy slid her hand up Sam's warm back. "I'm always willing to give my all for scientific research," she said happily.

He encircled a bare nipple with his thumb. "I like the sound of that. Give your all. Damn!" He jumped to his feet, grabbed the abandoned sweatshirt from the floor and threw it at Addy before hastily buttoning his shirt.

Addy sat up slowly, the sweatshirt held against her bare chest. "What?"

He thrust the hand that had so recently caressed her breast in front of her nose. "My watch. I just saw the time. We're getting married in a little over an hour and Emilie's still sleeping." He yanked Addy to her feet, the urgent air dropping from him as he viewed her state of half dress. "At least you're about ready to step into the shower." He slid his hands up her arms to her bare shoulders. "I'd like to step into that shower with you."

"Do you two think you could wait until after the ceremony?" Hannah's acerbic voice came from the hallway. "I came to tell you Mr. Burgess is coming to the wedding, and I reminded him he wasn't to breathe a word to Emilie until you say so." She shook her head. "I hope some day you two learn to close doors." The last words, said without much hope, came from down the hall.

"Do you have any idea how desirable you are when you blush?" Sam asked. "I'm looking forward to getting you behind a locked door and seeing your entire nude body without interruptions." He laughed as her blush deepened.

Addy's heart still raced as Sam turned in the doorway to blow her a kiss. She looked forward to seeing Sam Dawson's nude body, too.

Nude body.

Addy clapped her hands over her mouth and dashed to the door. "Sam," she hissed at his disappearing back. "Come here. Quick." As soon as he came close enough, she grabbed him, yanking him into the room, and closed the door behind him. "Did you find the necklace I made for you?"

"That's the emergency?"

"Answer me. It's important. Did you find it?"

"If you mean the one wrapped in Christmas paper with a big tag on it saying 'Mother,' yes, I found it."

"Did you really order it for your mother?" At his nod, Addy said, "You have to give it back to me. I'll make her something else. Something she'll like better." Much better, Addy thought.

"It's too late. She saw the package on my bed and waltzed off with it. I told her she was absolutely not, under any circumstances to open the package before Christmas."

Addy breathed a sigh of relief. "Good. You can steal it back, and I'll make something else."

Sam chuckled. "Knowing my mother, I'm sure she's already opened it." He hesitated. "I probably ought to warn you, Adeline, but my mother tends to be overly fond of having her own way. She says she's aggressive, but the truth is, she's downright bossy and can be a real pain sometimes. She takes after her mother. I guess it's a female thing," he said seriously. "My brothers and I aren't like that at all."

Any other time Addy would have fallen down laughing at Sam's incredible claim. Now all she could think about was the necklace she'd made.

"You OK, Adeline? You look kind of funny all of a sudden."

"I'm fine, just fine." Addy pushed Sam out into the hall and shut the door, sagging against the frame. Already she'd done something stupid to make her mother-in-law hate her.

On the heels of that thought came a more sensible one. Sam's mother hadn't opened the package. If she had, she'd have canceled the wedding. Addy looked at the clock across the room. One more hour. If Jo Jo Dawson put off opening the package for one more hour, then Addy would be marching down the chapel aisle. Jo Jo wouldn't stand up and object to the wedding. Addy crossed all her fingers. Sam's mother would wait until Christmas to open the package. Sam asked her to. And between now and Christmas, Addy could get the package back.

Jo Jo Dawson wore the necklace to the wedding. Addy's mother-in-law treated every guest at the reception to a close-up view of the roly-poly nudes dancing over the surface of each and every brightly colored bead. "I've always said Samuel is brilliant," Jo Jo bragged over and over again, "but he's outdone himself this time by giving me a beautiful, talented daughter-in-law and the most marvelous grandchild." She hugged Emilie who trailed after her new grandmother in stunned fascination.

"Our family was getting dreadfully dull. Medicine, science, business." Jo Jo shuddered dramatically. "I lived in terror Sam would marry someone I couldn't even talk to. You two—" she turned a ferocious scowl on Mike and Harry "—take a lesson from your older brother. When I asked Samuel if he loved Addy, he told me when she smiled at him, the feeling he got was better than a scientific breakthrough, or a first night opening on

Broadway. Oh, darn." She comically slapped her forehead. "I just realized. I wanted Sam to marry someone dumb enough so I could converse with her, and I just realized he married someone as brilliant as he is, if not smarter."

"C'mon, Mom." Harry, Sam's middle brother, winked at Addy. "You've always said Sam is the smartest person in the world."

"She's never admitted he can also be the biggest pain in the, uh, neck in the world," Mike, Sam's youngest brother, added, grinning at Addy.

"Exactly," Jo Jo crowed. "That's how I know Addy is so brilliant. She's smart enough to know how wonderful Sam is."

"And you two—" Sam glared at his brothers "—aren't to tell Adeline any different."

Sam's father, Martin, encircled Addy's waist with his arm. "This is my first chance to welcome you to the family, Addy. I've been telling Jo Jo and Mother Hannah for years, if Sam is as brilliant as they claim, he'll find the perfect woman for himself without any help from them. Thank you for proving me right."

Before Addy could set him straight, Sam's warm hand covered her mouth.

"As Adeline would be the first to tell you, Dad, it was just a question of finding the right candidate to fill a key position." He moved his hand, his eyes gleaming down at her. "Isn't that right, Adeline?"

"Absolutely." She looked at Emilie swinging from Harry's hands. "Emilie, when is your fifth birthday?"

"Ten days."

"And what did you tell me you wanted for your birthday?"

"A great big, big, big chocolate cupcake."

Everyone looked puzzled and intrigued as Sam warned, "Adeline, you wouldn't dare..."

"Emilie, before you walked down the aisle with the rose petals, what did I tell you I was giving you for your birthday?"

"Sam!" Emilie shouted. "My very own great big, big, big chocolate cupcake."

"Well, Cupcake..." Addy turned to Sam. "I'd say I found the right candidate to fill the key position, wouldn't you?"

"A toast to Addy," Mike shouted when the laughter died down. "Sam has finally met his match."

Addy opened her eyes. Moonlight showered the room and danced across the ceiling. Her thoughts skipped and jumped over the events of the day. A single day, just twenty-four hours, yet her whole life had changed. Emilie was spending the night safe in the bosom of her newly acquired large family. Emilie had liked Bill Burgess this afternoon. Soon Addy would undertake the pleasant task of explaining to her niece the newly-revealed relationship between Emilie and her grandfather. Addy's new mother-in-law had decreed Addy would become bead-maker to the stars once Jo Jo's friends had seen and admired her necklace.

Sam's entire family had opened their arms and taken Addy and Emilie in, welcoming them as treasures to be cherished, not burdens to be endured. And when Addy'd thanked Hannah, Cora, Phoebe and Belle for the support, the wedding, for accepting her and forgiving her her mistakes, they'd shrugged and told her that's what families were for.

Family. She'd become part of a wonderful one, thanks to one man. The pulse at the base of her neck beat steadily, warming the silver charm which nestled against her skin. "I love you," she said softly, propping her head up on her arm and looking down at the man sharing her bed.

The warm body beside her stirred. "I could get to like this," her bridegroom mumbled.

"Have I thanked you yet?"

"For what?" Sam rolled over on his stomach and laid his head on her chest. "For the pleasure we shared, or for locking the door," he muttered, "or for not divorcing you when you called me Cupcake?" A hand slid up her thigh.

Addy laughed softly, admiring the well-shaped head resting below her chin. "Those, too, Dr. Dawson. But right now I meant, thank you for yesterday morning, and for giving Emilie and me a family to love us."

"Adeline, a woman like you always has people to love you." He slid his hand higher. "In fact, if I weren't a scientist, and didn't know it was impossible to fall head-over-heels, crazy in love in three weeks, I'd swear I was in love with you."

Moving restlessly beneath his hand, Addy asked breathlessly, "How long do you think it takes to fall head-over-heels, crazy in love?"

"If I had to guess, I'd say about three weeks and a few hours." He coaxed the top of her breast into his mouth. Warm, moist air against her skin came with his next words. "I think the question calls for more scientific investigation."

The next time Addy awakened she was alone in bed. A rustling noise came from across the room. She raised her head. "What are you doing?"

Sam rummaged though his small suitcase. "I just remembered. As we walked out the door, Grandmother said she stuck a very special wedding gift in here." He extracted a small, slim box and walked over to hand it to Addy. "You want to open it?"

"If you'll help me, Dr. Samuel Dawson, Ph.D."

"Didn't I warn you what I was going to do if you didn't quit calling me that?"

She batted her eyelashes at him. "Aren't you the one who always says a demonstration is more effective than words?"

Sam pulled back the sheet. "I wonder if anyone has ever done a clinical study on the efficacy of freckles as an aphrodisiac?"

"Perhaps if you study the subject in depth you'll win a Nobel prize."

He slid into bed beside her, and slowly blazed a path among her freckles. "I won a better prize today." After a few minutes, Sam rolled off her and said, "Ouch." Reaching beneath his hip, he pulled out the slightly flattened box. "We still haven't opened this."

Dropping the ribbon on her chest where it curled around her nipple, he lifted the lid and frowned, pulling out a small roll of paper. He unrolled the sheet, gave it one glance and broke out laughing. Addy grabbed the paper.

Hannah had given them the letter Sam had received in Boston. Someone had written in spidery handwriting across the bottom of the page, "Some matches are made in Heaven. Others are made at your grandmother's bridge club." Hannah, Cora, Phoebe, and Belle had signed the note.

"The nerve," Addy gasped. "They're actually bragging about it. This ought to prove to you I had nothing to do with that letter you got. I don't even know how to play bridge."

For some reason her words made Sam laugh harder.

Addy rammed her elbow in his side. "It's not funny."

Sam leaned over her. "Addy maddy?" Before she could answer, he lowered his head. "Addy not maddy," he muttered against her lips, "because I love you."

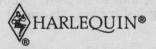

On the plus side, you've raised a
wonderful, strong-willed daughter.
On the minus side, she's using that
determination to find

A Match For
MOM

Three very different stories of mothers,
daughters and heroes...from three of your
all-time favorite authors:

GUILTY
by Anne Mather

A MAN FOR MOM
by Linda Randall Wisdom

THE FIX-IT MAN
by Vicki Lewis Thompson

Available this May wherever
Harlequin and Silhouette books are sold.

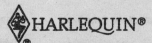
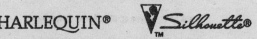

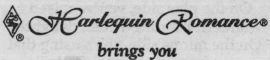

brings you

SIMPLY THE BEST

*Authors you'll treasure,
books you'll want to keep!*

Harlequin Romance just keeps getting better and
better...and we're delighted to welcome you to our
Simply the Best showcase for 1997, highlighting a
special author each month!

These are stories we know you'll love reading—again
and again! Because they are, quite simply, the best...

Don't miss these unforgettable romances coming to you
in May, June and July.

May—GEORGIA AND THE TYCOON (#3455)
by Margaret Way
June—WITH HIS RING (#3459)
by Jessica Steele
July—BREAKFAST IN BED (#3465)
by Ruth Jean Dale

Available wherever Harlequin books are sold.